WHAT WAS LOST

WHAT WAS LOST

UNDENIABLE TRILOGY - BOOK TWO

JOLIE MOORE

This edition published by
Moore Digital Media Inc
1125 N Fairfax Ave, Unit 46071
West Hollywood, California 90046

Cover: Najla Qamber Designs
Photo: Jenn LeBlanc Studio Smexy
eISBN: 978-1-944179-49-6
ISBN: 978-1-64414-033-8

ALSO BY JOLIE MOORE

What Was Perfect

What Was True

Taming the Bad Boy

Her Secret Crush

Fifty First Dates

CHAPTER 1

IT MADE my heart beat so fast it hurt when I thought about it.

That last breath.

Death.

What was it like? That instant when someone knows that those are their last moments on earth. My best friend, Liling, told me that babies take their first breath by sucking in air. That old people take their last breath by pushing air out.

It scared me.

Death.

I hadn't been allowed in the room with Grandfather Li. Children, "like me," my aunts had said, were not allowed.

My cousins had come, sat, held his hand, and left. I'd watched their shadows shift and move through the thin rice paper covering the door. I didn't know what made me different. What made me a child, "like me."

I *was* different somehow.

The one fact I knew better than I knew my own name

was that my mother hated me. She'd never treated me any nicer than she'd treated the helper who cooked the dead animals from the market and wiped dust from the floor.

I'd tried to change Mother's mind about me so many times.

I didn't get into trouble.

I got perfect grades.

I practiced my piano.

I perfected my English.

None of it worked. This week was just another in a long string of days when someone "like me" was treated differently from everyone else.

My grandfather's house was loud and quiet all at the same time. My mother and her sisters had walked around with their heads down whispering and murmuring for days. In between, a shriek or a moan would pierce the silence, only to disappear like smoke. Like the sound had never happened.

Until today, though, I'd never seen a dead body.

"We have to go, Jian. It's shou ling for Father," Mother had said.

Almost two weeks ago, the helper had pulled bags from storage and taken clothes from my room. My mother had called the school to get me excused. Then with her lips pulled tight and large sunglasses over her eyes, even though it wasn't sunny, she ushered me into our long black car. The driver took us three hours from our house in Shanghai to my grandfather's property in Nanjing.

It had taken nine days for Grandfather Li to die.

Mother and her sisters had walked from the room about

three minutes ago. It's how I knew he was dead, because no one had left him alone during shou ling.

I sucked in a breath and tiptoed down the hall. Sticking my fingers between the panes of the sliding door, I pushed them open a crack. Under a white sheet, with his eyes closed, lay Grandfather. I slipped through the door and took a step closer. I lifted the sheet just a bit. His skin looked like rice paper spotted with tea stains. What little hair he had left was flat against his skull.

What had happened to his hair?

Last time we'd been here, Grandfather Li had been sitting behind a large, intricately carved wood desk. Mother'd had her head bowed like she was praying at a shrine. Father had been talking a mile a minute about expanding his business.

When Grandfather had noticed me looking, he'd stood, slammed his hands against the desk and lectured my parents about manners. I'd slinked away, hoping whatever they'd all been talking about before I'd come in was more important than remembering to scold me later.

Then, his hair had been thick and black as night. His face had been unlined. It certainly hadn't had all these spots. I traced one, then another, surprised to find myself by the side of his pallet and touching him. He was warm; not warm like me, but not cold like skin after time in the winter cold.

"What are you doing in here?" my aunt Wang Fang screamed at me. I hadn't heard her come in.

"I...I wanted to pay my respects..." I stammered.

"You cannot be here. You're not supposed to be here."

"Because I'm a kid?" I asked. That's what Mother had

said when I'd asked her for the fiftieth time why I wasn't allowed. But three of my cousins had come in here. They were the favored cousins. My grandfather had pictures of them with my aunts and their fathers along the shelf in his office.

There were none of me or my father. Though I'm sure my mother had brought him the family portraits that we had to sit through every January, two weeks before we came here for the New Year. She always made sure to honor her father.

"Because you're not a Li. You will not be in line next to your mother at *jia ji*. You will be with your father."

I looked away from Grandfather and up at my aunt. Her face was even more cold and distant than my mother's sometimes was.

"I'm a Wu," I said. Grandfather Li had no boys. Only girls. My mother and my aunts. The other cousins who had been included in the shou ling vigil weren't Lis, either.

"Zhou Zhang Min and Wang Li Jie were here yesterday. Their last name isn't Li." I knew that my last name wasn't the answer, but I pressed the issue nevertheless. I was sick and tired of everyone tiptoeing around what made me—*like me*.

Exasperation or exhaustion or grief lined her face. Her eyebrows came down and her mouth pulled into a pinch.

"You stupid boy. You don't know, do you?"

"Know what?" My heart sped up. I could feel it coming after so many years. I was about to find out the truth about why I was different, why I was "like me." I braced myself, because I couldn't pick out of the known universe what the reason could be. I'd thought of and dismissed them all.

"You're the son of a whore." Her voice was harsh. Her

whisper a shout.

Before I could close my mouth, people I didn't know flooded the room.

"You must leave," a woman said. "We need to prepare the body."

With a wave of her hand, she ushered us out.

I looked at my aunt. She wouldn't meet my eyes.

Not needing to tiptoe anymore, I shuffled down the long hallway, then outside to the building where my mother and I were sleeping. I went into my room and sat on the bed, wrapping myself in the blanket there.

Was a whore what I thought it was? A woman who was dirty and poor? My father and one of his business associates had whispered the word when we were driving on the Huaihai Middle Road. Mother was anything but dirty and poor. Grandfather Li had been one of the wealthiest men in the province. Mother had always worn clean clothes.

Then it hit me with the force of a ten-ton truck. It all made sense and none of it made sense at the same time.

Mother wasn't my mother.

My face was round, not like my fathers, but not as thin as Mother's or that of my cousins. My hair had always had a slight wave she was forever trying to tame. My father and she had hair as straight as a stick. My skin was dark. Hers was light, pale, even when she forgot her umbrella and went out in the summer sun.

If Min Li wasn't my mother, then who was?

When my grandfather's coffin closed a few days later, the kid who I'd been when I'd come to Nanjing died a little inside.

CHAPTER 2

NOW

BELLA.

Bella was my weakness.

Bella was my past.

Bella was my future. She just didn't know it yet.

I was glad that her back was to me because I'd almost lost my shit the moment I'd seen her hair. Those dark brown strands that had brushed against my cheek so many times when we were kids.

My mind flipped like a Rolodex through all of the times we'd bent our heads together all those years ago. First, it was to conspire to skirt the strict rules my stepmother and her mother loved in equal measure, though they were by no means the same rules.

Then it was to get into mischief. Midnight swimming in the pool. Secret videogame marathons with a blanket tucked under the door to block out the light.

Later it was when I'd fallen in love with her, and we were in bed together, our bodies cooling from our first time.

It had always smelled like coconut, her hair. The urge to find out if it smelled the same nearly overcame me. Almost propelled me to do something indecent and inappropriate.

I thanked God that my conservative Chinese upbringing kicked in before my emotions did. I shook my head as if that would be enough to dismiss all those images of the past. The memory of that smell was enough to get my cock moving. I closed my eyes and willed the sense memory to go away.

The brand-new president of Woo DynoMedia—the company that had just bought one of the major three US television networks—did not walk into a conference room of his new acquisition with a hard-on.

With Bella facing the other way, it took me a full minute to realize that she was on the phone.

On company time.

The way she was hunched over, her arm flying out every few moments to punctuate whatever she was saying, suggested it was anything but a company matter. I didn't imagine that anything in her department inspired that kind of passion.

She pulled the phone away from her ear. It was a Blackberry. Anachronistic in Apple-happy Los Angeles. I plumbed through my mind trying to remember if transferring to Blackberries had been part of the deal I'd signed. I didn't think so. But it would have been a minor point in thousands of sheets of paper. I was a detail-oriented guy, but even I didn't catch everything.

But I caught a name when Bella whisper-shouted, "Daniel. I'm at work. Gotta go," into her phone.

That man's name deflated anything and everything

within a two-mile radius, and most certainly my dick. Nothing had changed. Bella was still a sugar baby with her billionaire sugar daddy.

I quieted the voice that pointed out the irony of the situation. That I wanted to take Daniel's place.

"Some things never change," I said, well before I thought better of it. I was always on the wrong foot with Bella. We'd been like two peas in a pod one day and oil and water the next.

No matter how hard I'd tried, we'd never been able to get back to that original closeness we'd shared. Half of it I knew was my father's doing. But the rest, that was on Daniel. He was the fly in the ointment with sticky feet, rubbing his bits together like a cartoon villain.

Faster than the speed of sound, the high-backed leather chair spun toward me. Bella jammed the phone into her briefcase as if her personal call would go unnoticed. Her face was a mask of guilt, then shock, or maybe surprise. If I hadn't known her more than half my life, I'd never have seen any of that. Because as soon as her brain worked through it all, her poker face descended.

"If it isn't the Wimpy Panda." After all these years, those were her first words to me. It wasn't at all the reunion I'd hoped for.

I'll admit those words hurt. She'd gone straight for the jugular with that one. Her tone of voice completely caught me up short. In one sentence, she'd blown my fantasy to bits. It's not that I thought she'd exactly fall into my arms. But we had...history. That had to count for something.

I buttoned then unbuttoned the jacket of my suit, unsure of which would make me more approachable. Bella stood. She was taller than I remembered. That made no sense though, girls...women didn't grow, not after high school. Then I looked down and saw that she was wearing heels that could pierce a man's heart. Before I could get a word out, explain why I was there, color rose high on her cheeks and she spoke again.

"What the fuck are you doing at CBT? Please tell me you're not pitching a show, 'cause you're totally in the wrong place. This is Program Practices. I'm about to start our weekly progress meeting."

I fingered the visitor badge clipped to my lapel, the sheen of the plastic shiny in the glare of the halogen lights. I looked at her, all buttoned up in a skirt so slim, I wondered how she walked. A blouse so white I imagined she didn't dare drink coffee. Shoes so high that they made her look like she could be pushed over with a feather.

I looked at all of what she'd become...and I wanted the girl back who I'd met when we were in middle school. The girl who'd worn baggy jeans and sneakers, overalls and hoodies. Whose clothes had been soft under my fingertips.

I called that girl's name. "Bella."

But that girl was gone to me. A woman who didn't love me looked at me with something like fear...no...defiance in her eyes.

I used that woman's name instead. "Isabella Aconi."

Her eyes roamed up and down me once again. This time they narrowed.

"Vice President, Program Practices." She said it like it was a hex she was going to put on me. Then she cracked the tiniest bit, running her fingers through her hair. Flawlessly colored and cut, it went back exactly the way it was designed to. Perfectly messy as if she'd just rolled out of a bed that happened to be in a Beverly Hills salon.

It was miles from the girl with the messy ponytail I used to tug. Acres away from the newly minted TV professional I'd last seen in Philadelphia seven years ago.

"Izzie. Isabella Aconi." I couldn't help the teasing tone in my voice. "Look at you, all grown up. All dressed up. It's like you're a bona fide adult."

If literal fire could have come out of her eyes, I'd have been burned for sure. I wasn't at all sure how we'd gotten here. She'd been my best friend when there weren't too many of those in suburban New Jersey willing to befriend a fresh-off-the-boat Chinese immigrant. She'd been my first love, if not my first lover. That last was tinged with years of regret. We should have been each other's firsts in everything.

"And it looks like you're still a bona fide asshole, Wu Jian."

It was like she'd channeled my stepmother, and not in a good way. Bella's use of my Chinese name in that maternal tone of voice scraped across my raw nerves like a bow across violin strings.

I swallowed, ready to defend myself. Ready to right this ship that was in danger of capsizing. I shifted in the suit jacket that was starting to feel like a straightjacket and I considered what approach would work best. What could I say that would bring Bella back to me? Erase all the bad that had gone between?

Her mother. She loved her mother. I'd adored her mother, for the most part. She'd been a victim of my dad just like everyone else under that roof. I was about to lead with that, when her phone rang *again*.

It had to be Daniel. There wasn't a single other person who had a hold like that over Bella. A girl didn't make it to Vice President while answering texts all day long. Daniel was blowing my plans all to hell. Hadn't been the first time.

"Since when do we use Blackberrys?" I sounded like the asshole she accused me of being, but I couldn't help myself. Daniel had that effect on me. Pissed me off more than any man on earth—except my dad.

Asshole Billionaires should be a reality show. Maybe I'd run upstairs and across the hall and pitch that one. Then I realized it had already been done to death on a different network. Maybe having money was inverse to having consideration.

"We? Is that the royal 'we'?"

It dawned on me then. She didn't know. She had no idea why I was there. Or who I was *now*. She still thought I was that kid who took orders from his stepmother, cowered at his father's commands, took it from bullies. Those days were long over.

"The network," I said, as if I were talking about God himself making phone-use policy.

"I don't know why you're asking about network policy. But if you must know, this is a private phone."

Then Bella took her eyes off me. Actually looked down at that damned phone again. She was good. I had to admit that. I knew her well enough to know that whatever she saw on that screen was pissing her off. But I'd seen her learn to craft her responses to her mother...and my father. She knew how to pretend nothing had happened even when an earthquake had shaken her very foundation.

Bella barely blinked as she tapped four keys and shoved the phone into her portfolio, but not before taking one last look. Her mouth twisted.

Daniel Van Dijk had just gotten an electronic middle finger. I'm not sure why that fact made a little bubble of hope lodge in my chest, but it did.

I searched her face. Looking for a way in. But there was nothing. It was closed as tight as a prison door. I knew one way to get a reaction. Maybe if I pushed a little, she'd open up. Maybe I could find out who she was now if I cracked the surface.

"You haven't asked about your mother."

Bella lost her poker face. I thought she'd come to me then. Commiserate like we used to. Like we had that night after it had all gone sideways. But she didn't move. Just swallowed. My reaction to her the last time her mother had come up had been all wrong. I was here to make it right. If I could.

Not *if*. I knew I could if she'd give me half a chance.

Then she could see that I wasn't that kid she'd met when I was thirteen, or the kid I'd been at sixteen, and not the asshole I'd been in Philly. Our last true encounter had been the worst. It had made my father's summons to China to "learn the business" all the easier to take while I licked my self-inflicted wounds.

"When's the last time you saw her?" They'd been close, Bella and Maria. They'd only had each other for so long that their relationship had to be one she cherished, now that we were all older and wiser.

I wasn't angry at my father any longer. Mostly I was resigned to the kind of man he was, flawed, but nonetheless brilliant for those flaws. With age, I was sure that Bella had reached the same conclusion. Forgiven Maria her trespasses.

"Been a bit. I'm sure all is well in Toms River," she said. "Nothing ever changes at Casa Wu. Maybe that should be Palace Wu now."

I knew Bella hadn't been back in years, but she and her mother must have been talking if she knew about the renovation. I didn't like it any more than she probably did, but I didn't exactly have a say in my stepmother's grandiose plans.

Min Li had ruthlessly bulldozed the houses that Bella and I had grown up in after she'd had a new fourteen-thousand-square-foot monstrosity built on the few acres we had in Toms River. No two people needed a house that big—or rather, no single person. Min Li was never in New Jersey anyway except as a place to store her haul from her Manhattan shopping sprees.

That house had been a big fuck you to my dad. As if a bulldozer could obliterate the years our parents had betrayed every one of us: me, Bella, Min Li, even Maria Aconi. It had to stop one day. Maybe not with a new house. But Maybe Bella and I could put a stop to that madness with *us*.

"She's thinking of retiring," I said. It was probably a

pipe dream. But I'd heard her say something to my father about that. The senior Wu had brushed it off. But my father and her mother would have to end their entanglement one day.

I fingered my lapels, wondering why in the hell her mother still bothered me. I'd accepted long ago that odd triangulation of our parents.

Why in the hell had I thought this would be the subject that would crack her open? If anything, it had made Isabella even more prickly.

"Maria Sofia Aconi would never retire," Bella said, confirming my worst fears.

"My mom brought a new girl from Nanjing." It was a half-truth. Min Li traveled with a girl. Bella's mom still did the major cleaning, but did not attend to my stepmom personally. At some point that had become too much.

At least I thought I'd accepted it—our parents' indiscretions. For some reason, I'd felt like we could never be together as long as our parents' infidelity hung over our heads. That couldn't matter, though. That could no longer be the thing, or one of the things, that kept us apart.

Father didn't matter. Neither my stepmother, nor her mother, mattered. Daniel didn't matter.

Bella looked me right in the eye then, unblinking.

"Cheap Chinese labor doesn't just affect factories, I guess. No one's job is safe."

Her zinger stung. I wouldn't have admitted that to anyone under threat of death, but there it was. I wanted us to be past this stage of hurting each other. It had to end sometime.

Before I could fix my mouth to soothe over those old wounds, my own retort popped out.

"My mom has gotten nostalgic for the flavors of home. She needs soups and vegetables, not pasta and cheese."

Food had always been a subtle tug-of-war between our families.

Bella didn't bite, though. Instead, she turned to the door as what I assumed to be her staff walked in. She turned back toward me, squinting in my direction as if I didn't exactly match up with her expectations.

"Jake, I don't know where you're supposed to be, or exactly why you're here, but I'm sure my assistant, Alexandra, can help you find where you need to go." Bella jutted her chin toward a young black woman who looked about five minutes out of high school, though she was probably well past. Isabella didn't appear to suffer fools.

Our long history cleared from my mind. Bella's offhand comment to her assistant confirmed what I thought when I'd walked in. Bella had zero idea who I was. For once, I had the upper hand. For once, I was in the driver's seat.

I widened my eyes just a bit and looked directly at the harried assistant. From the swift intake of her breath, I knew that *she* wasn't walking in blind. She'd read every memo that had come across her desk. If Bella ever fired this one, I'd hire her as my own assistant in a heartbeat. She was a bit of a disheveled mess, but her brain was sharp.

Breezily, Bella waved a hand toward Alexandra, the clanging of her bracelets the only sound in the too quiet room. "No worries, Alex," she tossed out. "I grew up with Jake in Toms River, New Jersey. We were...more or less...

next-door neighbors back then. There's nothing we haven't already said to each other."

That was the most truth that had been spoken in this room today. We'd said it all. Didn't mean there wasn't more to say.

Alexandra shook like a leaf, her head swinging between Bella's and mine. She whispered something. Bella shook her head, her movement's vehement. She was a woman who had clearly taken to being in charge and did not like to be questioned.

"What *about* Mr. Wu?" Bella said too loudly. The room seemed like it was getting even more silent, if that were even possible. "There's nothing you can tell me about Mr. Wu that I don't already know. We practically grew up together. I've seen him stumble his way through all the awkward stages of life. Looks like he still may be in one."

A current of anger underlay her words. Anger meant one thing: that she still cared. Hope rose in my chest.

I sat down in a chair, tilted it back, and put my black leather shoes on the conference table. This was going to be a train wreck. Isabella Aconi was going to lose her cool, and I had ringside seats. I couldn't remember the last time I'd seen her vulnerable.

"Ms. Aconi," Alexandra hissed. "I have to talk to you—about why he's here." The assistant was working hard to insert herself between Bella and the inevitable.

"Is it an emergency?" Bella's eyebrows kissed her hairline.

"No, it—"

"Spit. It. Out."

"The new network owners are touring today. This—"

"Ah, our new corporate overlords from China." Bella's eyes flicked in my direction. "First AMC Theatres and Dick Clark Productions. Now us. Should we hazard a guess about Woo DynoMedia? You think they're in the metals business or shopping malls? Because, folks, that's who *today's* Chinese billionaires are. Tomorrow, they're Hollywood's corporate moguls. God save us all from people looking for a little Hollywood magic."

Her little tirade went over like a lead balloon. I wanted to tell her that, like one of those bad insult comics, she'd lost her audience. I stood from the chair. It rolled back toward the wall with a near silent thud. It was now or never.

I buttoned my jacket, smoothing the fine wool.

"Good afternoon. I'm Jake Wu, President of Woo Dyno-Media, the new owner of CBT Network." I heard the shuffling of shoes down the hall and for the first time in my life was happy with my father's timing. He poked his head in the room. I waved and he stepped in, followed by five other of the newest board members in dark suits.

"This is my father, Feng Wu. He's the CEO of Woo DynoAutomotive. My family sells about four million vehicles a year to customers in China and around the globe. In today's interconnected world, we're looking to diversify, bring our shareholders and customers value.

"And we know you here at CBT are working hard to make the network accountable and keep the airways clean," I said. This speech was long practiced and perfected. "It was nice meeting you. I'll be learning from you, so I apologize in advance for my silly questions. In the next few weeks, I'll be by to introduce myself to everyone, but if you have any questions in the meanwhile..."

I gave out my new CBT e-mail address, nodded, then turned on my heel.

We did the same song and dance about ten more times in ten more conference rooms before we got to the top floor, where our newest board members had staked out offices.

I stepped into mine, a huge affair that overlooked low-slung sound studios and the slim trees planted to deflect the heat between the buildings.

Wharton hadn't quite prepared me for all that was involved in running an operation this diverse. Half our operation was on the East Coast, news and sports. Half on the West Coast, entertainment programming. Nightly news, morning infotainment, evening comedy and drama, and even a single soap opera still on the air, a throwback to a time long before I was born when they'd apparently filled most of daytime programming.

I had to review them all for profitability. Big decisions had to be made about what and who was going to stay or go. But I couldn't sit down, get my mind to focus on what was necessary.

There was a saying in Chinese that loosely translated to "if one walks by the riverside, one's shoes will eventually get wet." When I'd urged my father to let me try my hand at media. When I'd convinced him that an American company would be better than a Chinese one. When I'd pushed for a move to have our corporate offices mainly in Los Angeles over the traditional New York, I'd left out one glaring fact that I could no longer hide...

Bella.

Feng Wu hadn't so much as blinked in his few seconds in the Program Practices conference room, but he wasn't an idiot. A woman who'd practically grown up in our house, who'd lived on our property for years, would not go unnoticed.

I stood at my window, my back to the door, mentally counting down. I didn't even flinch when my door banged open with nearly enough force to break the metal doorstop screwed into the floor.

"Tell me that this fifteen-billion-dollar deal had zero to do with that girl," my father yelled in English.

Most of the other people he'd put on the board had passable, but not perfect English. They were Chinese billionaires who wanted exactly what Bella had said, a taste of Hollywood glamour. Feng Wu would not be humiliated. I was banking on it.

I turned, shoved my hands in my pockets, and looked him in the eye. I wasn't a boy any longer who could be cowed by words or threats. Or promises, rather, because my father did not make threats. He always followed through. I didn't blink when he tried to stare me down because I'd well known that a year of plotting, planning, and poring over documents would eventually come to this.

"You said yourself that owning an American media company was a good diversification idea." My response was as bland as I could make it. There was nothing in that sentence that my father could grab ahold of and turn back against me.

He shoved his hands in his own pockets then and walked

softly, deliberately toward me. Feng Wu stood next to me, pretending to do as I was—taking the measure of the hazy horizon beyond the low-slung buildings.

"Why did you break up with Liling?"

That question came completely out of left field. I'd geared up my brain to argue about the merits of CBT. Downplay the importance of Bella. But my father was no fool and had come at me sideways, blindsiding me.

I did the mental gymnastics of pulling together a whole different set of arguments I hadn't trotted out in some time. "I didn't want to marry out of obligation." That, at least, was the absolute and unvarnished truth. Being back in China had given me up-close and ringside seats to what would have been called arranged marriages at one time, but were now called marriages of convenience masquerading as love matches.

My father turned to me, lifted his hand, and started ticking off her salient qualities on his stubby fingers. "Her father owns Red Dragon Television. She was educated at USC, then the Synder School at Owen. Majored in Multimedia. She's trilingual, speaks Spanish, English, and Mandarin, all fluently."

"She sounds like an excellent candidate, maybe we should hire her here because"—I waved my hand over the stacks of papers and DVD cases on my desk—"it looks like I could use the help. You know what? She could head the Spanish-language division of CBT."

I was only half kidding. Liling was no one's fool. She'd make an excellent division head.

"She is pretty. She would have borne you many strong boys."

Because being a billionaire made you a genetics expert nearly rolled off my lips. But I was playing a long game. A very long game. I needed to learn to curb my impulses starting now, because I'd done a shit job of it downstairs.

"When? When she took a five-second break from the career ambitions all that education had prepared her for?"

"Did you not like her? You were engaged to her."

There had been so many mistakes with Liling. The most mature thing I'd ever done was to break off that engagement no matter who'd been hurt. We would, all of us—Liling, her family, mine—be better off in the long run.

"Father, this conversation is not about Liling. I don't doubt her father will be able to marry her off once he gives the matchmakers a list of her impressive credentials."

"Her father doesn't want her marrying some young upstart with no money." The fact that my own father said that with a straight face nearly knocked me on my own ass. But of course he had guile.

It was that and his stunning lack of self-awareness when it came to his personal life, that allowed him to become the ruthless CEO who'd had enough money, stock, and clout to turn a small appliance manufacturer into a major car manu-facturer, and in turn buy me this network.

My "What in the hell could go wrong with that?" ques-tion was immature, but growing into my adult self was coming along slowly, sometimes at a snail's pace.

"This conversation is not about your mother and me," he

said, this time his hand waving away his glaring infidelities like they were so many gnats.

"Stepmother," I ground out in English. There was no word for stepmother in Mandarin. It wasn't a concept the Chinese readily accepted. To the outside world, my mother was dead and Min Li had graciously stepped into her place. Calling her mother was supposed to show my gratefulness, deference, appreciation. I was sick and tired of so much damned gratitude.

"I'm not going to argue with you about Min Li, Wu Jian. Did you know that Isa...Iz... Maria's daughter worked at CBT?"

With this question, I was on solid ground. I'd already rehearsed my answers.

"I knew she worked in media. She was at an owned-and-operated when I was in Philadelphia."

"It doesn't matter. You have to fire her."

"What?" I pretended outrage. Getting rid of problems—and people who were problems—was my father's specialty. His request had been predictable. "She's been VP for five years. Her record has been flawless. In fact, ratings have grown with some of the envelope-pushing shows on at ten."

"You know an awful lot about it."

I sat on the corner of my desk so he could see the stack of papers that came up high against my waist.

"Everyone knows that, after acquisition, the first order of business is cut the fat. The second, increase profitability, if not that first quarter, then at least the first fiscal year. CBT is publicly traded, so there's no wiggle room here. I've reviewed nearly every department. There's a lot of fat. But the FCC practically mandates standards departments at every television network, even in basic cable."

"Hmph. Well, I don't want to see the two of you together. There's no reason for you two to work together, ever, is there?"

"I'm kind of busy here," I demurred. I wouldn't make promises I couldn't keep. "I need to get reports to the new board before half of it flies back to the mainland, so if you'll excuse me."

"I'm very serious about what I've said. You don't have to be president of CBT. I can replace you in a heartbeat. I hear that's how it's done all the time in television."

"You're reading too much gossip. Most presidents are forced out after a year anymore. Doesn't make for good television."

"You're not one of them."

I wanted to tell him all the things *he* wasn't: a good father, a loyal husband, an honest businessman. But saying none of that would advance my cause. I needed to play it all very close to the vest.

"Father. I will do nothing to embarrass you. Now, if you don't mind..."

He took the hint, walking through my door and closing it. The minute I heard his feet shuffle away, I removed my giant Post-it from the back of my office door. I'd doodled on it this morning, but had forgotten to take it down. I did that now, carefully folding and tucking away the two-foot-by-three-foot lined yellow square.

Had my father turned around, looked over his shoulder, or slammed the door on his way in, he'd have seen two words at the top of the sticky note, "Bella Aconi," followed by my list, my master plan to get her back—and I'd have been royally fucked.

I looked at the miniature bamboo plant that had been a gift from a superstitious board member and bowed toward it solemnly.

Luck and fortune were on my side.

CHAPTER 3

TWENTY-TWO YEARS EARLIER...

"WHEN CAN I READ IT?" Liling asked. Her question kind of sounded like a whine. I tried not to be annoyed. She may have been a girl, but she was the only person who'd split manga contraband with me. Mother had threatened to send me away to a school for misbehaving boys if she caught me sneaking one of these books again. She said they were inappropriate for someone my age.

I wasn't one hundred percent sure Father would let her do it...Mother sending me away, that is. But I wasn't one hundred percent sure he'd stop her, either. As much as I hated being here, I didn't think some far-off school in some rural town with more pigs than people would be better.

"As soon as I'm done," I whisper-hissed at Jiang Liling. We were getting close to my house, and I didn't want anyone to overhear us or see us playing tug-of-war with the glossy paper cover. "That was the deal. Last month you got it first. This month it's my turn."

We were at my door, and I just wanted to go in. The cover of this one looked like it was going to be good.

"This is stupid. We should have gotten two," Liling said. I know she was trying to manipulate me. She was trying to use my fear of my parents to get me to hand it over. Then it might be a week or two or never until I saw it again.

Liling had a way of forgetting when it was my turn. She probably had twice as many hidden in her house as I had hidden behind the garden shed out behind our building.

"And get in twice the trouble? At least this way we make it less likely both of us will be caught," I rationalized. I couldn't see Mother or Father, but it was like I could feel them staring at me through a crack in the windows or through the narrow slit of glass next to the door.

"My parents are the worst." This was Liling's constant complaint, as if limiting manga was the worst crime a parent could commit.

I didn't say anything. Her parents were strict, but at least they loved her. When her father was being stern, I sometimes saw him smile when he didn't think we could see. I'd seen her mother scold her for not practicing violin. But then she'd run a hand through Liling's hair and lay a gentle kiss on her head.

It was those little acts of kindness that haunted me. That made me feel like something was missing.

What was missing, I knew, was my real mother. I'd never had the guts to bring it up to them. To ask them, if Min Li wasn't my mother, then how did I end up with them. Was my mother alive? Or was she dead? Should I be mourning?

"Do you think the girl on there is pretty?" Liling asked. There was an unusual hesitancy in her voice. She wasn't exactly the shy and reserved girl that she acted like around her parents, but she wasn't exactly bold, either.

The girl on the cover made me have all sorts of feelings, none of which I wanted to discuss with Liling.

"She's okay, if you like...well if you like orange hair and blue lipstick," I answered.

"Boys aren't interested in real girls like me," Liling said.

I nearly dropped the book I'd been holding so tight these last few minutes. My eyes snapped up to hers to see if she'd been baiting me, just to get me to give it to her. But all the laughter, teasing, and joviality had gone out of her eyes.

I blinked again and looked at her like a girl, and not like the daughter of one of my father's business associates who was, from what Father had determined, from a good enough family for us to associate with.

Liling had clear skin and intense brown eyes. Her hair was parted in the middle as always. But somewhere between school and our neighborhood, she'd pulled the band off that she used to keep it back. The dark brown waves spilled over her shoulders.

"You're fine. I've got to get inside before someone starts wondering where I am. I promise I'll get this back to you tomorrow, or Monday at the latest."

Liling's eyes fell from mine. She took in a whole lot of sidewalk before she nodded and walked past me. Her house wasn't too far from mine. I didn't watch her go. Instead, I took a deep breath and walked to my own door.

Maybe I'd been paranoid, because when the helper opened the front door to let me in, the house was eerily quiet like no one else was there. Usually Min Li could be heard giving someone orders on anything from how to clean my bedroom floor to the proper way to prepare crab.

From the quiet, I could only assume she wasn't home. I let the relief wash through my body, then nodded at the maid before going to my room. After I closed my door, I looked through my school books, pulling the contraband from the stiff nylon bag.

A few pieces of paper floated out. Instead of jamming them back in, I spread them around me so if anyone came in, I could slip the book under one of them and pretend I'd thrown papers around, frustrated by the hard math homework we'd been given.

I turned the first page of this new one called *Party of One*. The main character had unrealistic orange hair. I could never figure out what the Japanese loved about all the outrageous hair colors. Anyway, orange-haired Sakai was looking for his brother, who'd somehow gotten lost in some seedy neighborhood.

While he was searching, he got a new friend, Kokoro. She lived in a house downtown with lots of other girls who didn't seem to wear a whole lot of clothes.

I shifted a little, my butt moving involuntarily, causing my school papers to flutter. Something about Kokoro's tight clothes made me feel kind of tingly in my underwear. Then an image of Liling looking straight at me floated into my head, and I felt even more uncomfortable than usual.

Normally I could spend a good half hour imagining being in a house of girls without clothes, but I quickly moved past that section into the meat of the story. The feelings Liling was bringing up were too confusing for me to think about.

Instead, I focused on orange-haired Sakai, who was looking for his brother.

In a scene eerily reminiscent of what had happened to me in Nanjing, the boy, his hair slicked back in preparation for mourning, was being told that his mother wasn't his mother, and that he had a half brother who'd somehow been forced to move out when no one wanted to take care of him.

I watched the shadows grow long, knowing that any minute, someone was going to come in here and yell at me because I hadn't practiced piano. Because I wasn't downstairs writing out English paragraphs. But I couldn't tear my eyes away from the book. It was as if some outside force had glued my eyes to the page.

My stomach growled as Kokoro and Sakai were walking down every seedy Kyoto block they could find, looking for anyone who could help. They had nothing more than a fifteen-year-old photo and a gut feeling to go on.

I was rooting for them though, hoping they'd find him, and with that, a really good explanation of how a mother could let her son go. It had to be something good, like she'd been brainwashed, or maybe even the manga standby —amnesia.

"What's that you've got there? Son?"

My head snapped up when the lights in my bedroom flickered on. I don't know how long I'd been reading in the dark. Probably the streetlight filtering through the open curtains had been enough to keep me from noticing how much I had to squint to see the letters.

"I'm sorry," I stuttered. I thought about shoving it under the math papers like I'd planned. Instead, I looked my father in the eye. My voice when I spoke this time was calm, collected. "I borrowed it from Liling," I confessed, hoping that he'd go easier on me, knowing I'd borrowed it from a girl from a good family.

"It's okay. I was a young man once. It's the kind of thing we do. Just make sure your mother doesn't find out."

"I...uh..." I stammered. Not out of fear of punishment this time, but embarrassment. Those kinds of feelings. The ones that had me touching myself every morning. Burying scraps of tissue down deep in the garbage cans. Those weren't the kinds of things anyone talked about. Least of all with their father, while he sat on their desk chair, wrapped in a very imposing dark suit.

I made the strategic decision to pull the open book over my lap.

"Look," Father started, then looked anywhere but at me. "Boys are different than girls. They have to seek satisfaction often. There are different ways to go about that. Of course, by yourself at home is one." He turned in the chair and stared at me until I met his eyes with my own. "But if you want help, I can take you to a pink room where pretty women are happy to...spend time with you."

I think I knew what he meant. Boys at school had talked about this sort of thing. Their fathers taking them to the clubs around People's Square so they could become men. I didn't at all want to think about that. Not while my father was in the room with me.

Turning the subject to something that would stop that train of thought, I boldly asked, "Who's my real mother?"

"What do you mean?" My father's spine stiffened, his body becoming rigid in the chair. "Min Li is your mother."

"No, Father, she's not." I was done with this lie. I was done with all the lies. "I was reminded in Nanjing of what my place was. I thought it might not be true what...Mother... and her sister said. But when you came for the funeral and didn't object to where I was in the line, I knew it was true."

He closed his eyes for a moment. I'm sure he'd done the calculations of fighting Min Li for my proper place and somehow thought the snub would go unnoticed by me. Because what did twelve-year-olds know about funerals and customs anyway?

Chinese tradition wasn't something I paid attention to. It was important to the older generation, but not mine. Truthfully, I wouldn't have known if I hadn't been told. But once I knew, no one could unring that bell.

"It doesn't matter, Jian," my father said. He stood and jammed his hands in his pockets. Something he only did when my mother had her boss face on. "Min Li has raised you since you were born."

"She doesn't love me, though." That one I said barely above a whisper, because the fact that she wasn't my mother didn't make the fact that I was somehow unlovable less painful.

"Of course she loves you. Look at all she does."

What she *did* was arrange lessons, and school, and meals. It was the same thing my father's secretary could have done.

"She helps care for me," I admitted. "But that's not love."

"You are naïve, Wu Jian. Love is not the most important

thing in a relationship. Loyalty. Obedience. Piety. That's what's important."

"You didn't answer my question." I did not want him to leave this room without telling me the whole truth. Something told me this would be my only chance

"What are you reading about in that manga?"

It wasn't an answer. But I felt like I was close to getting one as long as I played along.

I closed the book and flashed the cover, explaining about the quest for the mother, skipping the half-naked-girls part.

"I think it's time I told you about your real mother," Father said, as if this whole conversation was his idea. But everything was like that. His ideas were brilliant. He didn't much listen to anyone else. Min Li sometimes, but she held the purse strings.

That was the second thing I'd learned at the funeral. The sisters had found their father's papers after the body was cleared away. There were a few mentions about what was going to happen to Grandfather Li's company and stuff.

Everything was split between the three husbands of the sisters. Except somehow, Father had to go through someone else from the Li family before he could make any business decisions. He'd been very angry, stomping around for a couple of weeks after that before he and Min Li had settled into some kind of truce after he'd announced a huge expansion, building a new factory out in the country somewhere, this one for cars and not appliances.

"So..." I prompted. He was staring somewhere in the middle distance. I could see that he was reliving some kind of memory. But he was neither smiling nor frowning, so I didn't immediately push.

"It's important in a marriage to be loyal to your wife, put her above all others. But like you're discovering..." He gestured toward my hand, which was too close to my crotch. I immediately snatched it back. I took hold of the book with two hands and shoved it under my pillow. "Men and boys have urges that women don't. I...made a mistake...had an indiscretion with a woman here in Shanghai. She got pregnant because...you know how babies are made, right?"

I nodded. Not one hundred percent sure of the facts, but I knew that a man and woman had to kiss and lie down together for it to happen. How exactly it got done, I didn't know. And I certainly didn't want to hear about the gory details from my father.

"So she got pregnant. But she wasn't married. She was in no position to have a baby. Her family probably would have disowned her if she'd had the baby there. She stayed here, and I helped her out as long as she agreed to hand the baby— you—over to us. A male heir is important, and Min Li is unable to produce a child. You can never repeat this to her, of course. I'm only explaining all this to you so that you understand that you were very much wanted."

"Not by...Mother."

"Min Li understood once all the facts were out on the table. Then she came around. Your mother has been ideal, never sharing the secret with you. I'm sorry you had to find out the way you did. We had no intentions of telling you."

"But how? I always knew I was different."

"Different? You have all the same opportunities of the richest boys in Shanghai your age."

"Where is she now?" I was embarrassed about the crack in my voice, but there wasn't anything I could do about it. I closed my mouth, held my breath, and hoped he would answer.

He didn't pretend to misunderstand. I was grateful. "In a town outside of Wuxi," Father said.

I calculated. She was probably no more than a few hundred kilometers away. Dad's driver could have us there by morning if we left now. Leaving now, though, to find her, to see her, to ask her why, was out of the question.

"Jiangsu province," he finished.

I sat with that for a minute, wondering if that was the origin of my name. Nothing about Father's face suggested I should ask that question.

"Do you ever talk to her?" I knew I was being stupid, but hope filled me like it did when I'd been a little boy waiting for my father to get home from a long trip abroad, exotic presents sure to be bulging from his suitcases.

He looked away, staring through the window at the lights along the Huangpu riverfront.

"Once a year I send her your school picture." He turned back to me. Pinned me with his eyes. I didn't dare move now even though I was starting to lose feeling in my butt and legs. "I've made one hundred percent sure that she's well taken care of."

"Do you think she misses me?" My voice was a whisper, quiet in the room. My father was silent so long that I could hear the cars outside, the hawkers selling noodles on the street, faraway ship horns on the water.

"She married. Had three more boys."

"Oh." I hadn't been expecting that. Somehow I had her living in a one-room house, sitting out among the chickens, her face windburned, looking forlorn. Middle-class mom who'd somehow gotten around the one-child policy was something different entirely.

"Our bargain was that she would not reach out to you in any way. Min Li and I would raise you. Give you every opportunity. Speaking of, I came up here because I have something to tell you."

My mind spiraled through hundreds of possibilities, not latching on a single one. "What's up?" I tried to make my voice casual, though Father's face was anything but.

"We're moving to America."

CHAPTER 4

TWENTY-TWO YEARS EARLIER...

I TOOK one last look at myself in the mirror. I was dressed in the American version of my Chinese school uniform—the tracksuit. Instead of nylon, though, this one was made of black cotton and had white stripes down the side of one leg, and a jacket that matched with a matching stripe down the side of a single arm.

I'd tried to figure out what the other kids would be wearing. From watching some of the television while I'd been here the last few weeks, it was obvious that fashion was important to American kids. Something told me that this black tracksuit would not be the best first-day outfit.

There was nothing I could do about it now, though. Dad had bought me five different tracksuits like the one I was wearing, and he'd considered his school clothes duty fulfilled after that.

I lifted my backpack, empty save for a few notebooks, paper, and supplies that had been dictated by a letter in the mail. Books, it had informed us, would be supplied by the school during the first week.

For a moment, only a short moment, I kind of wished that Min Li was here. She had a kind of second sense about all of life's situations. It was as if she'd gotten some kind of guidebook the rest of us had not. She'd have taken me to the mall here or in New York and would have gotten just the right clothes. But something had shifted after her dad's funeral...and she had only been here to New Jersey the one time to decorate, and then she'd flown right back home. I hadn't had the guts to ask if she was coming back.

"Ready?" My father's question was a command.

I snapped to attention, embarrassed to be caught staring in the mirror. "Uh, yeah."

"I'm still looking for a driver, so you'll have to take the bus home after school. Your Mandarin lesson should be in my office on the fax machine, so be sure to check that as soon as you get home. Also, don't forget to do your piano hour after your homework."

"Do you think there will homework on the first day?"

"This is supposed to be one of the best school districts in the tri-state area, so I hope so. Americans are lazy though, so even if they don't assign anything, you should start reading the books so that you're ahead of the rest of the class."

We got into his new car, one of the ones his new division was manufacturing in China. After I'd buckled myself in the passenger seat, Father paused before turning the key in the ignition and gave me a pointed look.

"I promise to practice Mandarin and piano when I get home from school," I said dutifully.

"Good. Good. You can't let yourself get as soft as the Americans. They don't try hard. In this land of opportunity, you can do anything if you work hard."

"Yes, Father," I said nodding. Then I tuned him out on the rest of the short ride to school. I'd heard the familiar rant several times over the last couple of weeks, since he'd caught me watching episodes of a show called *Home Improvement*.

He'd watched five minutes and declared the American experiment a failure. He'd stalked from the room mumbling that he'd probably be able to take over the automobile market in a matter of months if that's what he was competing with.

There were hundreds of kids milling about when Father pulled up to the low-slung tan brick building. My heart went into overdrive. I thought my English was good, but maybe not good enough to maneuver through all these kids. Where were the classes? Where were the teachers?

I glanced over at Father, but he was busy trying to navigate the circular drive where parents were dropping off kids. When it was our turn at the top of the arch, I slowly unbuckled my seat belt.

"Hurry," Father said in Mandarin. "There are many cars behind me."

I turned and saw a line of luxury sedans idling, so I pushed open the car door and stepped out. Before I could turn to say goodbye, Father was gone around the curve and back onto the street, his stoplights barely flashing before he made a left.

Shrugging my backpack onto my shoulders, I turned and did the only thing I could do, walked into the crowd, scared as a new puppy in a new house. All I had to do was not pee on the rug.

"Hey, who's the new kid?" I heard from behind me. In less than a second, two boys had bracketed me—one on either side. They were smiling, but in America, that didn't mean they were nice. Americans smiled at everything, all the time. It was hard to tell what the feeling was behind it.

"Evan," the other kid said, shoving me into Evan.

"Cole," Evan said, pushing me again, sandwiching me in the middle.

"Jake," I announced trying to take all the jostling while not falling over into the wide, curved expanse of sidewalk. No matter where I was in school, Shanghai or New Jersey, I knew I'd never live it down if I hit the ground on the first day. It was better to be forgotten than remembered for something stupid.

"Where are you from, Jake?" The way Evan said my adopted name, I knew that my American English pronunciation hadn't been nearly as good as I'd thought.

"Shanghai."

"Shanghai," Cole said in an exaggeration of my Mandarin. "Do you mean Shanghai?" he drawled the question, lengthening the pronunciation like most did here. Made them all sound like they were from Texas to me.

"It's southeastern China," I said. Though if you'd asked me, I couldn't have told anyone why I'd said something so irrelevant.

"Have you seen any pandas? Are they out roaming through the woods or something?"

"In the zoo in Beijing." I nodded. "Maybe they have them

wild in a bamboo forest or something. I don't know. I lived in Shanghai. It's a city like New York." This time I was far more careful in how I pronounced my hometown.

"What else do you have in China that we don't have here?"

There were a thousand answers to that question. I didn't think they were actually asking what they were saying. Americans said one thing and meant another. It was something that my ability to speak English didn't help with at all. It was like the constant smiling.

"The Great Wall," I said after too long a pause.

"Right. I hear you can see it from space," Evan said.

"Yeah, it's pretty cool. One of the world's biggest man-made structures."

"I think that's the only thing that's big in China." That was Cole. I understood every word, but still was having trouble keeping up with the back and forth.

"We may not have the Great Wall, but at least we have big dicks," Evan said with a whoop of a laugh.

My brain whirred through all the words I knew in English, but I couldn't place it. Dick. I thought it was a name. I think it was a president. But I couldn't figure it out. I spoke before I could think not to.

"Dicks?"

Evan looked at me. "Cock."

"Cock?" I echoed.

Cole looked at Evan, then me, then said, "Hose."

"Hose?" I looked between them. Somehow the joke was going to be on me.

"Johnson. Junk. Nut cannon. One-eyed snake," Cole said.

"Pearl diver. Porksickle. Schlong. Pussy poker," Evan countered.

"Sausage roll. Shaft," Cole added.

It hit me like a stone against my head. It was a penis. A damned penis. I tried to remember how the conversation had started.

"If he doesn't know what those are, then they are definitely dickless in China," Cole said.

There were over a billion people in China. How did they think we got that many? Sex wasn't something everyone talked about like here, where everyone on TV seemed to be hopping in and out of bed with each other. Even the teenagers on that series set in southern California were doing it.

"We do okay," I stuttered. "A billion worth of okay."

"Have *you* done it?" Cole pointed at me, his finger quickly coming close enough to stab me in the chest.

I looked between them to see if they were serious. I knew everything down there worked, but that didn't mean that I could imagine actually being with a girl...like that.

"No. I'm thirteen. You?"

Evan and Cole smirked at each other and nodded. Boys were the same everywhere in the world. I'd bet all my English words and a bunch of Chinese ones that they were lying through their teeth.

"Older girl on the shore this summer," Evan said.

"She did us both," Cole joined in.

"At the same time?" I blurted out the question. Immediately I put my hand up to my mouth. There was no way I should have asked that. But the image made my thirteen-year-old brain work overtime.

"No way. We're not homos." They shoved each other. I was glad they weren't shoving *me*.

"You should come down to the shore. Marcella might be willing to make an exception and do you," Cole said.

"An exception?"

"Tiny dick and all," Evan said.

They both laughed as if that were the biggest joke in the world. The doors opened then and students started pushing their way in. I let myself be caught on the wave.

I'd looked at my penis in the mirror after the bath last night, when I'd been thinking about the Demi Moore movie *Striptease* that I'd snuck into. It had seemed like the normal size, especially when I thought about that one scene.

What they were saying couldn't be true. I mean, every man in the world had to have a regular-sized penis. Some people maybe got bigger or smaller. Some people were tall and others short. But just because lots of Americans were taller, didn't mean that they had bigger... Dicks...that had been the word they'd used.

I was wondering who I could ask, how I could find out, when a big shove against my back had me falling to the floor. My backpack hadn't been zipped too tight, so a bunch of pencils spilled out.

"Who's that?" a girl asked as she scooped up a pencil that had rolled half the vestibule away.

"Just the Wimpy Panda." Evan couldn't stop laughing at his own joke.

The girl laughed and repeated the nickname. Until six hundred kids were laughing and repeating the name over and over again.

Just like that, I was on my way to being known for something stupid. I'd probably be the Wimpy Panda for as long as I was here.

CHAPTER 5

TWENTY YEARS EARLIER...

"CAN I WATCH A MOVIE?" I asked my dad. I was standing as far from him as possible, practically holding on to the doorjamb for support. I'd walked by his office at least three times. Each time he'd seemed more preoccupied than the last. When he was busy, it was the best time to ask for things. He was likely to say yes and forget about me for a few hours.

"Come on in, Wu Jian. I want to show you something."

I swallowed deeply. All I wanted to do was watch *First Strike*, the new Jackie Chan movie. Dad wanted me to be fluent in English, and I was, almost. But living life in a second language was exhausting. I longed for a couple of hours where I wouldn't have to think. Where I could just enjoy the movie and not have to figure out the jokes behind the words.

"There will be time for movies later," Father said in Chinese. That was his standard answer about anything fun.

Later.

Work now. Fun later.

I wanted to ask him what would happen if I died before I got a chance to have all the fun. But I knew better. That would make whatever lecture was coming stretch from one hour to two.

I shuffled into the room and stood next to his desk.

"Do you see her?"

I looked at the paper, confused. Usually he was showing me spreadsheets or projections or engineering drawings or prototypes, while I wished I was the kind of boy who liked gadgets or machines or cars. I closed my eyes then opened them again, trying to figure out what I was looking at.

"Who is that?" I asked. He was holding someone's CV and there was a color picture clipped to the side. I squinted because the picture was passport-sized.

"Maria Sofia Aconi. I think she's going to be our new housekeeper."

"Oh. Okay. I thought maybe our helper was going to come from China."

"Wu Jian. China and America don't exactly get along. If we hired someone from Hong Kong, maybe. But the Chinese can't just hop on a plane and fly over here."

"Can't you just get someone from Chinatown?" We'd had a couple of women from there helping with the cooking and cleaning. None stayed the night, though, like in Shanghai.

"That's been fine as a stop gap. But I need someone long term. We need someone to keep this house clean and cook. Our American partners here don't want Chinese food they can't understand during meetings. This woman"—he tapped the paper—"is Italian American. That's the most popular food over here. Clients and investors will love it."

"I was hoping to watch the new Chan Kong San movie," I said, using the name that Jackie Chan did in China. I didn't much care about household staffing.

"Maybe later. You're going to need to help me with this interview."

I looked around to make sure Father wasn't talking to anyone else. I couldn't think what I'd know about interviewing someone. How did you ask them if they could shop and cook and clean? It seemed like a job any woman could do. Maybe not Mother, because she didn't do that kind of thing, but practically anyone else.

"You need me to translate?" I asked, already exhausted at the thought of spending an hour going back and forth between Mandarin and English.

"No. My English is fine," he said in English in an accent so thick, I wondered if this woman would understand anything.

"So what do you need me to do?" I was itching to get that tape in the VCR, the remote in my hands. The longer I stood here, the less likely I'd get to finish the movie before he found some new chore for me to do. Or remembered that I hadn't practiced piano yet or that I was behind in my Mandarin. Or that I hadn't practiced any of my ink brush calligraphy that was supposed to be my artistic outlet, because piano certainly wasn't.

"There's a girl coming with her. I want you to keep her from getting underfoot."

"A girl, Dad? This is going to be so boring. You expect me to play with dolls with her or something?"

"She's about your age. I don't know. Entertain her. If you

can keep her busy, you can skip piano today and watch that movie you want after she and her mother leave."

It was the fairest deal I think he'd ever made with me. Maybe he was softening from dictator to democrat on this side of the Pacific Ocean. I nodded my acceptance and ran from the room before he could change his mind. I needed to get the tape out of the shrink-wrap plastic and cued up in the VCR. Because the minute these people were gone and I'd slurped through dinner as fast as I could, I'd totally watch the movie not once, but twice if I could get away with it. School hadn't started yet. I could practice piano two hours and double up on Mandarin tomorrow.

I'd just managed to watch some of the previews when Father's voice crackled over the intercom. The girl was here. I was to come to his office immediately.

He'd had the squawky boxes installed everywhere in the house so he or my mother could summon anyone at will. I hated them with a passion, but obeyed the directives that came through them like the dutiful son I was. I ran down the hall, trying not to let the wallpaper make me too dizzy. Mother had gone overboard in her attempt to imitate American décor. It was the biggest mistake I'd ever seen her make.

She'd layered paisley over stripes, blue over gold. Then added a large dollop of traditional Chinese furniture shipped from her dad's house.

It was all a bit dark. Made me long to run outside. Dad had bought enough land to have a farm, even though there weren't any animals like there would have been in China.

Instead there was a swimming pool, an empty barn, a garage, and a couple of smaller houses. The gardener and his wife lived in one. The other was empty. If this girl was any fun, maybe we could do a race around the—

My fantasies came to a screeching halt when I rounded the corner into the office. An older woman stood there all buttoned up in a white suit and stockings, like she was interviewing for the role of nurse instead of housekeeper.

Next to her wasn't a girl in sneakers and jeans, like all the other girls in America. This one had on a pleated dress with puffed sleeves and shoes so shiny, I could probably have seen my reflection in them if I looked, which I didn't.

"Wu Jian." Father's use of my name brought me up short. I snapped to attention, making sure my hair was out of my face so I could look my father in the eye in the way he preferred. "This is Isabella." That part was in English. Probably for their benefit.

I looked away from Father and back at the girl again. Her brown hair was loose around her face. She ducked her head just a little bit forward and it covered her eyes and cheeks. In that moment, I had just the merest pang of sympathy. I knew what it was like to want to hide behind a mask, shrink from a new and unfamiliar world.

When I tuned back in, my father was telling me to get the girl something to eat and keep her busy until he was done with her mother. I looked at Isabella and saw this time what I hadn't seen before, that she was painfully skinny.

She looked like one of those beggar kids you'd sometimes see on the Bund who were nothing but bones, even though there were food-seller carts all around. You could see them, hand out, hoping for enough coins to turn the smell of noodles or fried dumplings into a real meal. Father never gave them anything. He said that the government provided for them. I wondered if the government in New Jersey didn't make any arrangements for Isabella.

"Follow him, Isabella." My father's voice was unusually kind, but Isabella came to me obeying the command it was. Her eyes gave her away, though. The tough exterior cracked and the tiniest sliver of fear came through.

"I'll be right here," her mom said.

I turned and strode through the office door. Standing in the room with mother and daughter made something gnaw at my stomach. It wasn't hunger exactly, but nevertheless, I really wanted to get some kind of food into the girl.

"You hungry?" I asked, not because I couldn't hear her stomach rumbling all the way from China, but because I didn't want her to think I pitied her—though I did. Of all the things I hated about my life, being hungry wasn't one of them.

"You speak English!" Isabella looked at me, her eyes going wide with shock. I could see it now. The hunger making her edgy. The fear that she'd have to spend an hour doing some weird pantomime of language with a guy who only spoke Chinese. I swallowed a laugh.

"Of course. Why wouldn't I?" My voice broke on that last word, and I ducked my head. I wanted my voice to change already. Instead I sounded like a dying walrus. It was a full one hundred and eighty degrees from how I imagined myself —a younger version of Tony Hawk.

"Um, your dad spoke to you in Chinese," she said.

"Mandarin," I corrected.

"What?" Her dark eyebrows nearly rose to the shorter hair framing the top of her face.

I sighed because I think I'd explained this once if not a thousand times in the last year. "Mandarin. It's the dialect. There are a lot of Cantonese speakers in New York and New Jersey," I said by way of explanation. "I asked you a question," I said pointedly. My voice was sharper than I'd meant it to be.

"I could eat, Wu Jian," she said, stumbling over the pronunciation of my name, doing a not-great job of imitating my father.

"Sit there." I pointed to the green marble table that was too big for the room and out of place in this country of smooth brown wood tables. "I go by Jake, by the way." The best advice I'd gotten from a friend at school who'd spent time in San Francisco was to pick an American nickname. It would, he said, make things easier for me if teachers and other kids could latch on to something familiar. He'd only been half right.

"Okay, Jake." Isabella shifted on her feet like she was nervous or hungry, or maybe both.

When I'd come home from school when we'd been in Shanghai, our housekeeper used to smile big when she gave me after-school treats. Sometimes it was noodles and broth, or dumplings. On an especially good day it could be lemon tarts or spongy rice cake. Until this moment, I'd never understood what that smile had been about. Now I knew. There was a certain satisfaction in feeding a hungry person.

I got a bunch of plates and bowls and put them on the table while Isabella busied herself at the sink with soap and water. One by one, I filled the dishes with steamed rice, xiao long bao, tofu flower soup. Then I went back for the green ceramic pot that lived on the back of the stove, its bamboo handle partially unraveling every time I lifted it, and poured tea for the both of us.

She hesitated for a bit after I pulled out chopsticks for us both. I didn't want her to think I was watching her eat because that was all kinds of weird, so I helped myself to a little bit of everything. It was good, hearty food. I looked at the soup again, then realized it was probably too weird for her as she sipped hesitantly.

I don't know where the impulse came from, but I had to poke at her when she asked, "What's this?"

"Duck blood soup." I waited for her to spit it out or at least make a face, but I got nothing. Instead, she took a bigger slurp than even I would.

"It's good."

"You heard me, right?" I put down my dishes and looked her fully in the eye. She didn't flinch. Admiration for her shot through me, making me feel a bit warm and uncomfortable at the same time.

"Have you ever had sanguinaccio or biroldo?" she asked, her accent strong on the foreign-sounding words. Some of the people I'd met here in New Jersey sounded like newscasters. The rest sounded like her, their English salted with a twang that none of my Hong Kong tutors had.

"What's that?"

"Blood sausage. Sanguinaccio is salty. Biroldo is sweet, like with raisins and stuff. Unless you have a dead human in here"—she lifted a single metal chopstick and pointed it in my direction—"I've probably eaten it all."

Mother would have fainted from Isabella's etiquette. Despite knowing better, I couldn't help myself and lifted my own chopstick in her direction.

"Aren't you going to have rice?"

That. Rice, not blood, stopped Isabella in her tracks. She paused an overly long time. Her face went from tan to red. I wondered if it was the heat from all the food. There was lots of steam in the room. Then I looked again. I think she was embarrassed.

I just waited because I couldn't begin to guess what she was thinking. Finally, she brushed her hair back from her face.

"I can't use chopsticks. Okay? I grew up with regular stuff...knives, forks, spoons smaller than the bowls they go in," she said. She'd dropped the chopsticks and was waving the long-handled soup spoon around. I resisted the urge to ask her to put it all down. Instead, I did the thing our house-keeper had done for me when I'd been very small.

I rolled my chair around and took her hand in mine. I almost dropped it the minute a shock ran up my arm. I looked around, searching for the source of the electricity. This had only happened to me in the winter when the static built up after scraping my feet along the rug. I looked outside to double check, but it was the usual warm sun. A breeze shifted the broad-leaf trees.

"Did you just joy buzz me?"

She'd felt it, too—the shock. I tried to place the current moving through my body with some experience in my past.

But the feeling was entirely new, and I had no idea what to do with it. I stood stock-still until she jiggled our joined hands.

"So..."

That snapped me back to reality. Right. She was a mess with chopsticks. I'm pretty sure there were western utensils somewhere here. I just had no idea where they'd be. It was the kind of thing that was saved for entertaining. Rather than scramble to the dining room, I decided to go ahead with my lesson.

"You do it like this." I put my fingers directly where hers were and showed her how to wield the metal sticks like little pincers. Isabella dropped them a good five times before I realized that my impromptu lesson wasn't working.

I closed my eyes for a second, trying to remember if the kid chopsticks were here. I jumped up and rifled through another drawer until I found them. The red plastic contraption was shaped like a long English letter "M."

Her face turned tomato red again. I wondered why she couldn't control that. School had to be hell on her if she couldn't keep the blood out of her face. Or maybe she didn't care because she had a huge group of friends who kept her safe from the mean kids.

"Are those for kids?" she asked.

That was it. She didn't want to be treated like a little kid. I looked at her again. She was likely older than she looked. I could see now that being super skinny made her look younger. But she probably wasn't more than a year below me in age.

"My mom got them for me when I was little, probably."

That was the world's biggest lie, but it wasn't everyone you told that your mother didn't love you or wasn't your mother.

I huffed out a breath, pushing through the pain that had lodged itself in my chest. It never went away, that pain. Just hurt more some days, less others.

"Where is your mom, anyway?" the girl asked, looking around as if Min Li was going to materialize.

"Nanjing." Somehow Mother hadn't really come with us. She'd blown through the first couple of weeks picking this crazy-making wallpaper and arranging furniture, then she'd flown back to China. Was staying in her father's old house. Part of me was relieved that she wasn't here dictating every single thing I did. The other part was sad that the buffer between me and Father was gone.

"Oh, that's nice," the girl said. I could tell from the way her face was screwed up that not only did she not have a clue what to do with the kid chopsticks, but she had no idea where in the hell Nanjing was, much less China.

My annoyance at her ignorance gave way because Isabella smelled incredibly good. I couldn't exactly say what it was, but I wanted to be closer to her. I decided another lesson was in order. Not that she'd ever need it probably, but I wanted her to have this little memory of this time we'd spent together. I wouldn't forget it.

"Here." I took her hand again. Our hands stopped shaking once they had each other. "These have like a little grip thing on them to help you pick up food," I said, clicking the serrated red plastic tips together.

I helped her pinch the thin skin of a soup dumpling. She moved it to her plate as slowly as a building crane moved a huge slab of concrete toward a high-rise. My breath caught in my throat, and I let go of her hand as quickly as I'd picked it up and rolled my way back across the table.

She tried to be delicate, but I think hunger overtook her. Once she got the hang of the kid sticks, she ate the dumplings and rice with enthusiasm. Not once did she wrinkle her nose at the different smells or tastes like I'd seen other Americans do.

Ten dumplings in, she finally slowed and looked at me. I didn't want her to be embarrassed again, so I searched for something that I thought we could talk about that wasn't food or hunger. I landed on video games.

"You play Phantasmagoria?"

Her eyes widened and she leaned across the table, bringing her that much nearer to me. I could see that I'd shocked her. Like everyone, I'm sure she saw an obedient Chinese boy who spent the whole day studying or practicing a string instrument. Instead, I wanted her to see who I really was, cool skater boy who knew his way around a video game.

"Your mom lets you play that?"

At her question, I sat back. Reassessed. Maybe we had more in common than I'd first thought. I'd yet to meet an American kid who seemed to have any kinds of rules at home.

I didn't think it likely that Dad would come in, but I wanted to keep my secret nonetheless.

"She's not here." Looking around the kitchen, I leaned in conspiratorially. "I rode my bike to the mall with Dad's credit card and bought it. It's really good." When the house was quiet and everyone asleep, I was trying out a bit of newfound freedom. No one had responded to Dad's ads for a live-in—

well, until Isabella's mother. Without someone always at home, I was able to get away with much more in America than I'd ever been able to do in China.

"Can we play?" she asked, her eagerness bubbling up between us. That unfamiliar itchy-in-my-blood feeling rose up between us again, but I tamped it down. I had to remember she was just a kid.

"Might as well," I said, then stood up and started walking toward what Americans called a family room. When I didn't hear anything, I looked behind me. She was tiptoeing like a villain about to get caught in a crime. When we got to the room, I pulled a joystick and controller from a cabinet under the huge TV set. The whole room practically pulsed with excitement as Isabella vibrated in the small space.

"Do you have brothers and sisters?" she asked. It was the first thing a lot of people asked. In America, it seemed like living in a big house was often equated with having a big family.

A small jolt of yearning sucker punched me. I'd half wanted a brother or sister growing up. Someone to be a buffer or go-between or just be on team kid versus team parent. On the other hand, I wondered, if Min Li could have had her own natural child with Father, would they have kept me? Or would I have been some kind of orphan on the street? One of those kids no one wanted that the government pretended didn't exist even when you could see them begging near the Bund.

"It's only me. One-child policy," I said, making it sound like a hard-and-fast rule even though I'd met my friends'

brothers and sisters, who mirrored the thousands of excep-
tions the Party made.

"What policy?" Keyboard forgotten, she screwed up her
face in question.

"China only allows parents to have one kid." I mimicked
the Party line.

"Seriously?"

"Yes."

"What if there are twins or something? Does someone
kill the second kid?"

"It's China, and not barbaric like that." Although maybe
it was barbaric like that. Since I'd been in New Jersey, I was
having a hard time wrapping my head around my country of
birth. On the one hand, we had ancient dynasties and had
invented two things that had changed the world forever: gun
powder and noodles. And on the other, I'd heard whispers of
people in the countryside killing their girl babies or aban-
doning them at orphanages.

"Twins are fine," I explained. "And if you only have a
girl, you can also try again for a boy."

"Why? What's wrong with having only a girl?" It was
funny how much Americans pretended boys and girls were
the same, even though they didn't act that way. There weren't
any girl presidents or girls running companies like Father.
The faces were whiter here, but that was the only difference I
could see between men and women in my country and hers.

The men had it much rougher in China. But I didn't
want to get into any of that, explaining how we were otherwise totally different in our obligations, the Chinese and

people like her. How we had to support not only our parents, but our wives and any child we had.

"Let's just chalk it up to it being a different culture. Alright? Boys have a big list of expectations that girls just don't have. They have it easy in a lot of ways. Now, let's play."

The minute the nude woman woke from her on-screen nightmare, I regretted choosing this game. Even though she had a sheet pulled up, it was no work for my imagination to fill in what wasn't on screen with flashes of skin and flesh that seemed to come standard in American movies.

Then the guy in bed with her, whose hair was too long and whose chest was too hairy, was promising her he'd protect her always. Then they were doing it.

I tried to stay as still as possible so Isabella didn't notice how uncomfortable all this made me. My father repeatedly talked about how boys had these kinds of feelings. How there were women who could help us out. I risked a glance at Isabella and she looked nearly as uncomfortable as me. This made me as squirmy as all Father's talks did. Did girls have these same feelings? Father had never said anything about that.

I was so grateful when the scene ended that I jumped into the first puzzle with more enthusiasm than I'd ever felt about a game before. A puzzle was something I could under-stand. Could share with this girl. Those other feelings...I just wanted them to go away sometimes. Other times I willed them to come and touched myself in a way that felt better than anything else in the world. I shook my head and focused on manipulating the buttons on the left and right side.

"Wu Jian!" my father yelled before walking into the TV room.

"Sorry. I...uh..." Isabella stuttered out then jumped up and dropped everything like the plastic had caught fire in her hands. My father for once had the grace not to point out her nervousness. I'd watched him do it with others, mostly to get them off-kilter so that they'd agree to whatever he asked.

"If your mother accepts my generous job offer, you'll be living here," Father said to Isabella with a courtliness I'd rarely seen from him. It must be what had worked on my mother and Min Li. Until this moment, I'd wondered how he'd won them over with a perpetually pinched face and puckered lips. "Wu Jian and I will show you the guesthouse," my dad continued.

I flicked off the set not just to hide what I was doing from my dad, though I could tell he wasn't paying attention at all. But I turned it off so I could listen better to what in the heck he was saying about Isabella and her mother living here in one of the other houses on our land.

We'd had live-in women before in Shanghai. But they'd always been Chinese and understood their place in the hierarchy. There was something about Isabella's mother that said she didn't understand. I don't know if it was her American-ness or how, despite the fact that she was small and thin, it felt like she was bigger than life, that they'd somehow take up more space than our helper had in China.

Like we were lined up at school, we all followed Dad from the house and through a winding path on the property to the one unused guesthouse on the land. Dad jiggled with the lock a second before the door pushed open.

Isabella and her mom went in first, but I made sure to follow close behind. The girl's eyes opened as big as saucers. I realized just then that if she was hungry, she may not have much of a place to live, either. The house seemed small to me. Just two or three bedrooms that I could remember, and an American kitchen and living room. Maybe one bathroom and that was it. The only time my parents had stayed in any place that small had been a hotel room in Philadelphia, while Mother had been working on making the New Jersey house what she'd called habitable.

"It's small and needs a good cleaning, but here it is," Father said while standing in the entryway with all of us. Mother and daughter walked in opposite directions exploring the house. Father looked at me with a smug, self-satisfied smile on his face.

Isabella came back and actually bowed at my father not once but twice, like she was auditioning for some weird Japanese kabuki. I wanted to poke her and tell her to stop, but Dad made a face like he kind of enjoyed it. The whole thing just made me feel really uncomfortable.

While Isabella was bowing her way out, Father pulled her mother aside and they shared a few words back and forth that I couldn't hear nor understand. Something was weird, off, but again, I couldn't put my finger on it. Maybe it had been that, in Shanghai, Mother had been in charge of all of this kind of stuff. Maybe it was weird that my father was hiring someone. Although he must do it all the time in his job. I mean, he ran Grandfather's business in China. Then he'd started making cars. He'd had to open a factory and hire a whole other group of people to do that.

Father showed them out with me bringing up the rear.

After their mess of a car sputtered, nearly died, then restarted and pulled away, my father pulled the guesthouse door shut hard and pocketed the key.

"And that's how it's done." He sounded practically triumphant, like he'd won a race or something.

"How what's done?"

Father paused for what felt like an overly long time. "Hiring someone to take care of things. This Maria," he started, the American name unfamiliar in his mouth. "She'll drive you to school, pick you up, and keep things clean here. Maria will cook as well. She's Italian, so you'll probably like that."

He was, of course, referring to my newfound love of pizza and pasta with cheese sauce. It was one hundred eighty degrees from anything I'd ever eaten in Shanghai. Cheese wasn't a thing in China.

"So about the movie?" I prompted.

"Go on. One lesson a day is enough I guess."

Before running off to put the video tape in the machine, I threw a look at my father. I wasn't sure what lesson he was talking about, but his permissiveness was fleeting. I was sure I'd get a longer lecture on whatever he was trying to teach me on another day.

CHAPTER 6

NOW

I SLIPPED the vibrating phone from my jeans pocket and had tapped the green answer icon before I'd thought much about it. Since I'd had my first phone when I was sixteen, I was in the habit of answering Liling's calls. She was the first person, other than my parents, to have my phone number, to have called me.

I remembered thinking that first Razr phone was magic. I remembered thinking that a girl like Liling falling for a guy like me was magic, too. Like first world humans' fascination with phones, my fascination with Liling had worn off long ago. Both were just an ordinary part of life these days.

"Come out with me, Jian," Liling was saying. I wasn't even sure I'd said "wèi" or anything at all, but she was talking a mile a minute anyway. "I'm having a party in Malibu. You haven't been to see me since I got here. The pool is amazing. From the sand, it looks like it's spilling over into the hills. When the lights are on at night? It's incredible," she said.

"Americans call it an infinity pool," I said. I looked out

the window of my apartment, checking to see if I'd missed something. But I hadn't. It was still light out. People were walking to and from the farmers' market and the mall and just wherever. Whatever was making me uneasy was coming from inside me. I looked away from the window and turned my focus to the woman on the other end of the phone.

"Liling...Lily, I have to work," I said on a sigh. Liling was exhausting sometimes. She wasn't as bad as some of the fuerdai. It wasn't twenty-four-hour parties and shopping while snapping pictures for WeChat or Instagram. But in her own way, she was quietly insistent. Or, as she was coming across in my ear, loudly insistent.

"On a Friday night? I find that hard to believe. You own a network, Jian. I could only imagine that there are thousands of people who could cover for you. What are you doing, anyway?"

What are *you* doing, I wanted to ask. After a couple of months, I was still unable to pinpoint exactly what Liling was doing in Los Angeles.

There'd been some talk from my parents or hers about her studying film. But Liling already had an undergraduate degree in film and a Master of Fine Arts from Owen, of all places. I fifty percent suspected that her mother or Min Li had suggested that she come here to keep an eye on me to make sure I didn't go too far off the rails...like dating a non-Chinese American or by getting married to someone who was not her.

Everyone wanted Liling and me to marry. For a few years, we'd both thought that was the direction we were heading in. She'd been working for her dad developing foreign television shows, while I'd been working for mine learning the Woo businesses from the ground up. But the spark had never been there. Or if it had, that spark had been manufactured by proximity, by parents, by circumstance, by our teenage libidos.

The thought of the day I'd decided to end it between us could still stop my heart. It was by far the worst sin I'd ever committed. What kept me from more guilt was that at least I'd prevented a greater sin of marrying someone I wasn't in love with. It would have been colossally unfair to her...to us both. For all my mistakes, missteps and faults, at least...at least I hadn't walked her down the aisle.

"It's the first big music awards show under our reign, so to speak," I reported back. For both of us, business and family came first. She would surely understand my obligation. Not question my ulterior motives. Not even assume I had any.

"Oooh. Awards? As in red carpets and famous musicians?" she cooed.

I hated this persona she took on. She was not one of those shy, retiring girls most Chinese parents preferred by any means. But she wasn't one of those girls who charted her every move on social media, either. Something about her pretending to be one of those kinds of girls rubbed me the wrong way.

I didn't have time to deal with her, though. I was here in Los Angeles for a single reason, and I needed all my wits about me to focus solely on that. Liling's party persona I could tackle on another day.

"There will be that, I guess." I hoped my answer was a

non-invitation, but I didn't have much confidence she'd read it that way.

Liling's "Then count me in!" was unfortunately predictable.

I tried again. "What about your party?"

"I can have a party on any given day. It's not like everyone isn't available at a moment's notice. It's only the difference between locations. It could be at Onyx with bottle service. Or at Laurel's with them doing shots off nude models. Or it could be here. One group text and the party moves to wherever the party is."

"Um." I was out of deflections and excuses. If I protested too much, her mother or Min Li would be all over us in a heartbeat.

The last thing I wanted right now was parental scrutiny into my love life or the apparent absence of one. If Father told Min Li about Isabella. If Min Li mentioned I was very much single...a conversation between them could spell disaster for me. Bella could be fired. Min Li might show up with a long list of women I should pursue. Liling was the lesser of those evils. If she reported back to her mother that we'd gone to this show, and it filtered through to mine, it would put a lid on that one for at least another month or more.

"I'll be at your place. What time? Four? Five?" she asked.

"I'll be downtown by then," I said. I rubbed at the place between my eyebrows that was starting to pulse with the start of a headache. Then I gave her the directions to the network's temporary on-site office.

"Four. I'll be there at four. It'll take me that long to pick the right dress and get down to you from Malibu. Why are you living down there anyway? You could have a house anywhere. With privacy. Not having to share a pool or a front door. I mean, you're next door to a mall, so there's that. But the Grove doesn't have any of the good luxury brands. Tell me that you're not buying clothes from the Gap or Top Shop something."

"It's walking distance from the network. A takeover is a lot of work. I don't want to be driving when I could be working."

"Right. I get it. Sure. I've gotta go now. See you in a few."

I'd have skipped the red carpet but Liling had knocked on the network's temporary on-site office door behind the theater before I could escape.

"Liling." I tried to make my greeting enthusiastic.

"Lily. I'm Lily in the States."

"What did you do, come by helicopter?" I joked. "Malibu is easily thirty miles and an hour and a half away on a Friday night." I'd been waiting for a call from her telling me that she was stuck in hopeless traffic and would turn around.

"Guilty as charged. I barely had time to get this dress on and make a couple of calls before I had to head over to Camp Eight. Can I use the bathroom? Where is it? I need to add a little lipstick."

I'd been joking about the helicopter. I should have known better.

"Lily. I have to go," I yelled through the hall toward the closed bathroom door. "The pre-show starts at five on the dot." Now that she was here, I wanted to get going. Get the public part of this "date" over with.

"One more minute."

I tried not to tap my foot. Instead, I buttoned and unbuttoned my suit jacket. I looked at myself in the entrance-way mirror the network set up to make sure no one encountered the celebrities with broccoli in their teeth. The midnight-blue suit skirted the line between day and night.

"Why aren't you wearing a tux?" Lily asked when she swished back into the room.

Lily looked amazing in a sheer black dress that seemed to cover everything critical but revealed all the rest.

"I'm working. A tux doesn't really cut it."

"What are you doing? Laying cable?"

I held back from laughing at her unfortunate use of words. "I'm going to be in the booth." I tried to keep my voice as neutral as possible. I wanted it to sound as boring as dust so she wouldn't ask to join me or for a behind-the-scenes tour. Although I was thinking that hooking her up with some kind of all-access pass to the stars' dressing rooms may not be a bad idea.

"What booth? I thought this was strictly an audience thing? It's not like the Golden Globes is it? I can't eat in this dress." She followed me with mincing steps down the metal utilitarian stairs.

"Control booth. I need to keep my eyes on what's going on behind the scenes."

"These people have been running a network for like eighty years or something, right? What can you tell them that they don't already know?" Once downstairs, I started walking around the back of the theater. "Wait. What are you doing? Where's the car?"

"A car? It's just a short walk around the theater complex."

"I can't walk in these shoes." She stopped dead and lifted the sheer fabric of her dress, revealing black pumps that had spiky heels at least five inches high. She lifted a leg, revealing a bright red sole as smooth and shiny as the leather on top. "These aren't walking shoes. These are sit-in-a-chair-and-look-beautiful shoes."

"Did you expect a car?"

"The heliport was too far away. I can't walk up to the red carpet."

She had a point. I'd planned to use my employee badge to swipe my way through a side entrance. I fished my phone from my pocket and clicked the Uber app. "Will a...seven series BMW be okay?"

"Fine. Fine. I can't believe you don't have a limo. You bought an entire network. It has to come with a limo."

I thought about it for a long second. She was right. It probably *did* come with a limo. I'd have to look into that for a drive longer than a half mile. I turned toward Olympic, where the app said the car was waiting. I lifted the handle and shuttled Lily into the backseat.

"This address, right?" The driver tapped at the screen on his phone. "I'm driving around the corner?"

I reached into my breast pocket and extracted my wallet. "Here's a tip." I handed over a hundred. The ride would now total one hundred and thirty-five dollars.

"I'll get you there in five."

And he did. We turned onto Chick Hearn Court in less time than it took for me to fiddle with the seat belt. I let it snap back into the pretensioner and stepped out and onto the carpet. Lily was firmly at my side. Only two of the fifty or so reporters recognized me. I smiled, nodded, and pretended that English was not a language I knew. They quickly shuffled away toward the men with long hair and shredded pants, the stars who would be on the stage.

"Here are my tickets. I'll join you when I can," I said, pressing the slim pieces of paper into her hand.

Lily was too busy smiling, her lips a ruby red I hadn't noticed before. I could see nearly every reporter looking at her, then looking at the others waiting for a cue, second-guessing themselves. They weren't sure if Lily was someone important or famous enough to approach or not. When she turned her head as if she were going to walk away, flashbulbs popped and the reporters swarmed en masse. She absorbed the attention like a queen.

She was annoying and demanding and a whole lot of other adjectives, but I answered each and every call from Liling. I had mad guilt for stringing her along for as many years as I had. Mad guilt. Like Bella, we'd been friends, then a whole lot more. Treating her as anything more than a friend had been one of the worst things I'd ever done. It was a crime I'd be paying for, for many more years to come.

Any residual guilt about my real reason for being there evaporated in a heartbeat. Liling or Lily would be just fine.

I followed my original plan, let myself into the cavernous building, walked around the back of the stage and took myself to the booth.

I'd talked to Connor, a CBT loyalist—or rather, a Connor loyalist. It sounded like my Bella was a bit of a micromanager. The woman on the button tonight—Bronwen or Padgett, some name that screamed boarding school and old American money—was new on the job and needed to be supervised, according to an e-mail she'd sent to Connor. When he shot back a missive letting Bella know he was otherwise engaged, she was quick to take over the show's supervision herself.

My father's advice would have been to let the girl with the WASPy name sink or swim. He swore employees didn't learn until they faced true consequences. Bella wouldn't be here long, though.

I wasn't like my father, or Daniel, for that matter. I didn't want the woman I loved to be beholden to me as an employee. Holding someone's livelihood in your hands wasn't love. It wasn't even very good foreplay. Bella and I would both quit CBT then live as equals while we figured out where to go from here.

Shaking off thoughts of how I wanted this to go in the long run, I walked into the air-conditioned and empty booth. No one was there, save for a dark-haired girl who looked like she was studying for a very hard test. I looked around though, and it appeared from the monitors and coffee cups scattered about that they'd set up, but the room was mostly empty. Probably out getting more coffee or smoking. Most importantly, there was no one there to ask me questions.

I lifted my eyes and thanked the heavens for the moment of silence. Such an American thing to do. Next thing I'd be doing the sign of the cross like the kids did in Jersey. The dark-haired girl was looking nervous. She had a sheaf of papers around her and was highlighting like she was cramming for a final exam and didn't notice me. I was about to introduce myself to her...again. I was ninety-nine percent sure that she was—

"Daisy." Isabella flounced in. Subtlety had never been her thing. It's one of the things I'd always loved about her. She lived big. Had loved big. I was counting on that big heart of hers to welcome the mature me, who was ready for a big love with her.

"Isabella," her employee started. "I've got the rundown here. Over the last week at home, I've watched the tapes of the last four or five awards shows on CBT, and a few on the other networks where there was crossover with who was going to appear tonight. I flagged the bands and presenters who are likely to cause any issues. Yesterday, I practiced on the Futterbutton. I can catch ninety-two percent of errors in five seconds or less, leaving two seconds to spare."

"What about the other eight percent?"

The girl called Daisy—I guess I'd been wrong on the name—turned as bright red as the soles of Lily's shoes. "I figured I'd use the extra two seconds. The odds of something happening are really small."

"Really small is not zero. That's why I'm here, Daisy. To eliminate that eight percent."

"Right."

I looked from one woman to another as the rest of the sound engineers and segment directors came into the room. Bella stood in the back of the room. Watching her would have been weird, so I turned my attention to the spectacle of the awards show rehearsal in front of me. Looked like more dry ice and sequins than actual music. From years of practice, I was a fairly proficient pianist. I'd had more than my fair share of recitals. This was a whole different level of performance.

The phone buzzed in my pocket. It was probably the fifth

or sixth time. I'd ignored it too long. I slipped the glass from the silk liner of my pocket. It was Liling, of course.

"Where are you?"

"Backstage," I hedged. I cupped the phone with my other hand to keep our conversation quiet. "My first awards show. I have to shake hands, make nice. Don't want everyone at the network to feel like we're so foreign. From what I read, there was a lot of resentment with the Japanese takeovers in the eighties. People were worried that they'd lose their culture. That's a bigger issue now with everything that's going on in America with Chinese trade."

I paused. I was both lying and telling the truth at the same time. And like any person who lied, I was talking way too much. If Liling knew that Isabella worked here, she'd be back here in a heartbeat to keep me on the straight and narrow path. Whatever happened, I needed to keep the two women apart. If they met, there'd be far too many questions I did not want to answer.

"So let's meet after. There's a new place in Hollywood, Adults Only, and a speakeasy in Fairfax called No Name. It's in your hood, so you should go."

Took me a minute to place the word "speakeasy." I think it was something from America's prohibition era, but decided not to get too deep into that with her.

"We'll do it. I'll text you when I'm ready. I'll meet you by the back entrance to Studio Four. I'll alert security." I hung up then texted Father's assistant to make sure that Liling had all access.

The sound of a thud on delicate equipment pulled my attention back to Bella. Not that it had ever really strayed far.

"Hey, watch it." I looked around to see that a sound engineer was giving the death glare to Bella.

She barely looked up from her other phone to glance at the engineer.

"I promise not to damage anything precious."

I watched the girl I'd loved for years. Something had made her hard. I wanted to...no, I needed to find the girl I used to know under there.

My only solace between bands and stars that were trying too hard or not at all was that Bella wasn't immune to me. When she thought I was busy, she snuck looks at me from under her lashes. Then she swung her long, lean legs from the board and stood. I wondered if she was going to find privacy to text Daniel. I was one hundred percent sure he hadn't left her life. I wanted him to be gone, but all the signs were there. The second phone. Her exasperated sighs at the Blackberry screen alternating with that expression that said she had a secret.

"Daisy, you got this? I have to take a call from the network."

I wanted to cough bullshit into my closed fist.

"Who's calling?" I was the network, and I wasn't the one pinging her phone.

Bella's eyes widened just that little bit that said she was caught in a lie.

She lifted her silent iPhone in the air and practically ran from the booth. "Gotta take this." Bella was surprisingly more agile in her mile-high shoes than Liling.

"They're closing with that hair metal tribute band,

Revival. From what I hear, they're clean," Daisy shouted to her retreating back.

I looked at the screen and wondered not for the first time about Americans. Fire and sparks shot into the air. The rockers' hair added about ten centimeters to their height. Between that and the sparkly boots with heels, they were a sight to behold. Even after all these years in the US, I still didn't understand the country's fascination with ordinary people dressed up in costumes. All the sequins and glitter on men moved them into idol territory. China hadn't yet moved into the cult of celebrity. We were starting down this road, but hadn't gotten to this degree yet.

I refocused on the bevy of screens in front of me when the room got surprisingly quiet. For a long moment, the only sound was of Daisy bashing at her button and gasping like a dying fish.

There, front and center on every single screen, was a penis.

I squinted to make sure I wasn't hallucinating. But there it was, blue and green and purple lights highlighting that the bass player did not have a bass in his hands anymore.

Frantically I scanned the screens, looking not for what was on the stage, but what was going out on the network feed.

I finally found the screen in the top corner by its "live feed" label. I had no idea who was in charge, but heads were going to roll. Because instead of a shot of the host or a black screen, the stage was still front and center.

The only saving grace was that three or four network suits had rushed the stage and were standing in front of the musician.

I stood and shoved my pinging phone into my pocket and rushed out. I needed to protect my father's investment at all cost.

This was my first nearly solo mission with Woo Dyno-Media and I'd fucked it up royally. My mind wandered all over the place, looking for a solution, because if I knew one thing, it was that my father would not grant me a second chance.

CHAPTER 7

NOW

BY THE TIME I ran out front, the action had moved from the stage to the dressing room. I found an empty chair and stepped up on it so I could see everyone and be heard.

"What in the hell just happened back there?" I yelled at the sea of suits.

Bella stepped forward, a little bit away from the crowd of men in wool.

"Blue happened," she answered.

I racked my brain for a good second, thinking of the meanings of the word blue. I didn't have the time to figure it out.

"Blue? Who? What?"

Bella blinked slowly. "Indigo Hawk? Goes by Blue. The bass player for Revival decided to play a different sort of instrument."

Was she joking? I'd known this woman nearly all my life and sometimes she had the worst timing.

An older white man split from the crowd coming to stand

right in front of Bella. I wished I was better with names and faces, but the last few days touring through the network had been a bit of a blur. I stepped down from the chair, but still had front-row access to Bella's dressing down.

He was pointing a finger at Bella's chest, though.

"When we hired you," he started. "When we hired you, we had two requirements." He brought his hand back and held up two fingers like Bella hadn't graduated third grade instead of Ivy League Owen. "Two things that could not happen at this network. No George Carlin and no Janet Jackson."

To her credit, Bella didn't look the least bit intimidated.

"It's not like we administer a drug test before performers come onstage," she was saying. "Not a single one of them would pass any kind of screening anyway."

She had a point. Drugs were illegal in China and they were illegal in America. In China, drug trafficking could get you the death penalty. In America, for anyone with money, it was for all intents and purposes legal. In entertainment, many used alcohol and other substances quite liberally.

I turned when everyone else did. The guy, Blue, whose penis had just been on display, had pulled up his rhinestone-studded pants.

"Hey, man," he slurred to no one in particular. "I'm not a druggie. I have a medical marijuana prescription. My bud-tender gave me a pre-roll of Green Crack. Must have been super potent."

I tried to follow, but thought the bottom line was that he was blaming his little performance on drugs. I was starting to think Bella was wrong. Maybe we *did* need to start screening the stars before they took the stage. I made a mental note to explore that policy with Legal once Bella somehow got this one squared away.

"So potent you unzipped your pants?" Bella asked, cutting her gaze in such a way that broadcast her disbelief.

The rocker hung his head just a little and let a sheepish grin split his craggy face. "Yeah, well. I was kind of in the moment. Made me horny as shit. This babe put her tits on the stage—"

"Okay, that's enough." Bella's hand slashed the air. "Rehashing isn't going to do anything. Thanks to Ms. Jackson and the Moral Majority, we're looking at a fine of at least..." She hesitated a long time.

Years of working with my father paid off in spades, because I was able to make the calculation of our potential liability within seconds.

"Three hundred twenty-five thousand dollars...per station," I said, emphasizing the vast amount her department's negligence was going to cost the network. Fortunately the network only owned a small percentage of stations outright. The rest of the affiliates we'd have to deal with on a case-by-case basis if they came to us hat in hand.

"Hopefully that won't happen." Bella plastered a smile on her face, as if that was going to be enough to erase the potential millions we were going to have to pay out. "This was more a Bono incident than a Janet Jackson."

I surveyed the faces around the room. No one looked like they believed a word Bella was saying. This was very much more like Janet Jackson than Bono in my opinion, but I didn't add my voice to the chorus that was going to rise up against Program Practices.

The lead singer of U2 had uttered a single bad word. Blue's penis was much closer to nipple exposure, minus the sunburst decoration.

I did another quick survey of the room. Bella was losing them for sure.

"I'll be here all weekend," she said. "Getting out in front of this."

Ignoring the hundreds of notifications on my phone, I brought up the calculator app. Before I spoke as the new owner, I wanted to make sure I had my numbers absolutely correct.

"We're talking a possible fine of nine million dollars, Isabella." She needed to know that no amount of smiling and kowtowing was going to be enough to erase this huge blunder.

Maybe if she'd been in the booth instead of running away to text with her sugar daddy, this wouldn't have happened. I had half a mind to ask her billionaire boyfriend to pay the fine. Fortunately, I was at an age where I could keep thoughts like that to myself.

Bella threw her shoulders back and stood even taller, if that was possible.

"Let's not jump the gun. No one's filed an indecency report. The FCC hasn't called. Let's go home, get a good night's sleep, and meet in the morning. By then, I'll have a draft letter for the owned stations and affiliates."

It sounded good, what she said, like a plan. Honestly, I didn't think it would be enough. Not in this day and age when everyone in America was sensitive to the smallest lapse in a man's behavior.

The notes were subtle at first. Then everyone quieted as they looked at their own phones or in their pockets to see if they were ringing. It wasn't the assigned iPhone's distinctive ring. It was the default Blackberry tone.

I couldn't believe he was calling Bella here and now. Did that man have no boundaries? Had she not established that she had a job to do?

That was just it. Bella had a job. I should know because I'd checked out her personnel file, and CBT had been signing her checks for more than five years.

No one was saying anything, so I took the lead again. "You going to answer that?"

She pulled out the phone, jabbed at one of the tiny buttons and stuffed it away.

"As I was saying. Tomorrow morning. Eleven o'clock. Fifth-floor conference room. Until then, gentlemen." She picked up all her stuff and walked right out of the room. Probably the right move. Otherwise, everyone here would have picked apart every one of the last moments Revival was onstage. She'd left when there was no way it was going to get better.

I paced backstage, patting a lot of backs and assuring everyone that the new owners of CBT had it all under control. I tried not to stew in the car on the way over from downtown to CBT. Turns out Liling was right, there was a limo at my disposal. Too bad she was missing out on the ride, but she didn't need to be involved in network business, the work side of what I did.

I marched up to Bella's office. I had to talk to her. At least I knew this much about her, that she'd be back in her office, trying to do damage control.

Curiously, her spiky heels were gone. I could see why she wore them, and the super-tight skirts. Without the height, she was much more vulnerable, approachable, neither of which probably squared with being an entertainment executive. I resisted the urge to reach out and touch her.

I could tell the moment Bella realized she wasn't alone. Her pivot was slow and deliberate.

"Don't you have somewhere else to be?"

Liling, then Father, flashed through my mind quickly. My former fiancée would have been happy to have me by her side as she navigated the awards show after-parties. From the number of notifications on my phone, Father was giving himself a coronary while he wondered if I'd just cost him millions of dollars. Money he wouldn't miss, but he looked at money like he was keeping score. I'd lost him a lot of points with this blunder.

The answer to her question was that I didn't want to be anyplace else. She wasn't ready to hear that, so I straightened my back and smoothed my lapels.

"The deal with Father was that I could straddle between daytime and evening programming, even stick my foot into news, but I'm being sidetracked by having to put out fires in Program Practices."

Bella took a deep breath, thrusting out her chest. I flicked my eyes away, keeping up the act that it was all business between us.

"Since you don't quite fit into the org chart here," she

started, her mouth pulled tight, "I'll give you the CliffsNotes version. The editions of the awards show that will air later or be repurposed for streaming have been edited to remove the genitalia, but still remain within time limits. We've got interns scouting the web for illegal copies of Revival's performance and we'll issue takedowns as they come up. Now I need to get home and get some sleep before tomorrow's meeting."

Like I'd ignored the way her deep breath pushed out her chest, I turned my traitorous mind away from thinking about her wrapped in her bed or in mine.

"What time is that again?" I asked. I wouldn't put it past her to exclude me.

Her "I'm sure you have something better to do" let me know she was planning on keeping me out of the loop. For the time being, I was going to be all up in her loop. But I let her walk away without answering, thinking she'd won that round. No matter what happened, I'd be where she was.

I made my way up to my office. Waited five minutes, then dialed Bella's true work phone. When the phone connected, I didn't wait for her greeting.

"Do you think Programming is overrated? Dad thinks that with my traditional Chinese sensibilities, maybe I should take a swing through Program Practices, see if I can set this ship right. I'm sure you'll find me an office."

I hung up, satisfied that she was clear that I wasn't going to disappear. For good measure, I sent her a final text: *I kind of liked your office. If you don't mind, I'll camp out there for the next few days. It'll be like old times. —The Wimpy Panda*

CHAPTER 8

EIGHTEEN YEARS EARLIER...

SOMEHOW I'D THOUGHT when Father had said we were moving to America that my life would be freer. I'd be like those kids on the TV shows I saw when we first moved. There'd be no parental supervision. I'd be down by the beach running around experimenting with alcohol, cigarettes, and girls.

Life in Toms River was very little like that. It was as if we'd just moved Shanghai, China, and all the expectations of the Han culture with us across the Pacific Ocean then across the vast land of the United States.

I was still expected to study Mandarin the same way I'd studied English. Piano was still an hour every single day. Homework came first. Fun came last if at all.

Tossing down my completed math homework, which was fortunately a few years behind my old school in China, I stood from my desk and stretched. My ears perked, but I didn't hear much of anything from the house. Min Li was in Manhattan. Father was probably napping. I poked my head out of my bedroom door, looking right and left down the long hallway, but there wasn't anything to see or hear.

I pushed the door back so that it wasn't exactly closed, but I'd be able to hear the click of the latch if someone came in. Then I pawed around under some shoeboxes until I found what I was looking for—the last of the manga I'd smuggled in from China. In the last year, I'd read them slowly, savoring them like Father did with American wine, opening one every so often.

This was one of the last I'd bought without Liling. It was one of the ones labeled romance, and probably for girls, but I'd bought it anyway and stashed it in my bag, then at the bottom of a shoebox before everything got packed for America.

The cover was typical, a brave-looking handsome guy holding on to a woman who looked like she needed protecting from the wind blowing through their hair, if nothing else. I sat on the floor, my back against the side of my bed, and started reading.

Instead of the characters being on some sort of quest or fighting evil, it was about a girl who sees demons—which are harmless until she turns sixteen—and the boy who protects her. This first time through, I was wildly impatient. I flipped until it was clear the two main characters were going to kiss.

I closed the book and stuck it between the mattresses.

Bella.

I didn't want to be reading about this stuff. I wanted to be *doing* this kind of stuff with Bella. Tell her how I was feeling.

In the last few months, something had changed. She'd

gone from being my best friend to a girl. A girl I very much wanted to smell, and touch, and kiss.

Fighting the urge to run, I tiptoed slowly downstairs and let myself out of the back door. Then I walked across the grass and around the tall pine between our houses. When I peered in Bella's room, I couldn't see anyone. Why wasn't she in there? Her mom made her study almost as much as mine did.

I slipped back into the shade of the tree and looked behind me. I thought I could see the shadow of Father pacing in his office. In just a few hours, he'd be on the phone to China after dinner our time, just when they'd started the workday there.

Then I saw her. It was her boobs, actually. They hadn't been there when skinny, underfed Isabella had walked into my kitchen that first day. But they were there now.

I'd spent an unhealthy amount of time thinking about the breasts that now sat away from her chest and the nipples that lay on top. She wasn't old enough to wear a bra all the time, so at home, she mostly took off whatever sweater or jacket she'd worn to school and was in a t-shirt that did nothing to hide her body. Today's shirt was thin blue cotton with white around her collar and wrists. There was a trio of colored bands around her upper arms and her chest, calling attention to what was underneath.

The need to be near her, maybe even kiss her, overcame me.

I bent and picked up a handful of gravel from the ground. I pinged one rock, then a second at her window. The third got her attention. She ran to the glass and pushed up the sill, but

I'd already let the fourth one go. Her hand went straight to her neck where I'd probably hit her.

I didn't mean to laugh. I really didn't, but the look of horror that marred her pretty face got to me.

"That's not funny." She leaned out the window, though her voice was still whisper-quiet. "You could have put my eye out." Bella had that look she wore at school when she was doing her Mafia princess act. The one I hadn't busted her balls about because it kept anyone from bullying either one of us. But in less than a second, the cracks came through. She disappeared as she bent toward the floor, and then my own forehead stung as the same pebble cracked me in the skull.

I walked closer to her window. The smell of the lemon soap she used wafted out the window. Between that and her chest pressing against her shirt, I was getting half a hard-on.

"C'mon," I whispered. I wanted to be alone with her, but nowhere near the house where our parents could come up on us.

She stood back from the window, throwing herself into shadow. "Aren't you supposed to be studying Mandarin right now?"

I ignored that twinge of guilt twisting my belly. Min Li was my problem, not hers.

"Mr. Chin is in China." My tutor had refused Father's offers to bring his whole family here, live on the property. He was back in Shanghai with his wife and kids this week. It was a great seven-day reprieve.

Bella shook her head so hard her hoop earrings swayed against her neck. "That doesn't mean a thing."

But she hadn't stepped back any farther into her room,

nor had she shut the window on me.

"It means that there's no one to tattle about me skipping out. C'mon, I want to show you something."

I didn't mention the something I wanted to show her was how my lips would fit over hers. I shook out my arms, trying to get rid of the nerves that were starting to scare me, making me think of chickening out of this stupid idea.

Maybe I needed to go back to my room and finish that book. Get some lotion and take care of myself. I was resigned to just that when she backed farther into the room. I heard a drawer slam, then she was back, leaning out, her hands on the outside sill.

I moved toward the bricks and stretched out my arms, my hands under her pits. She put her hands around my neck and, next thing I knew, I was lifting her out. I nearly dropped her, I set her down, then pushed her away as quickly as I could so she wasn't in touching range.

If she'd stayed close, she'd have felt my boner, and I wasn't ready for her to know about that. I wanted to get that first kiss out of the way. With all of our parents living in the same place, this was already hard. But I'd scoped out the shed earlier this week. The groundskeepers took Fridays off. Min Li was in New York. Dad was napping again or yelling into the phone, both of which made him oblivious to the world around him. Bella's mom was glued to *Oprah*. It was perfect timing. I didn't know when the opportunity would come around again.

I'd let go of everything except her hand. I jiggled it in mine. "Let's make a run for it," I said.

Gripping her hand harder, I pulled her and started

running. She kept up with me and we zigzagged across the lawn, around the covered pool, and toward the woods in the back. Out of breath, we collapsed against the huge roots of one of the trees.

"Think anyone saw?" Isabella asked as she scooted closer to me.

"We're clear. Your mom will be in my kitchen soon. My mom went to New York."

"What's she doing there?" Isabella asked, her tone full of judgment. I'd never shared the secret that Min Li wasn't my real mother. If I didn't think it would be disloyal, I'd have told her that I hated Min Li too.

"Shopping." It was one of three things she did. The other two were having lunch and thinking of awful ways to decorate the house that she hardly inhabited. Since we moved here, Min Li split her time between Nanjing and New York.

"So what's up?" Bella's question was so innocent when my thoughts were anything but.

With her this close, my breathing was anything but calm. I looked away, up toward the nearly bare tree branches as I tried to slow my heart. It was going to be dark soon, which meant dinner would be on the table. Maybe I could kiss her here. I was almost one hundred percent sure that no one could see us from the house.

I shook my head and stood. It was best to stick to my original plan.

I pointed to the cluster of buildings about halfway between the house and us. "It's in the shed."

"We should have run there first."

"It would have taken too long to map out the whole plan

while standing next to your window. I didn't want them to see us." I didn't have to describe who "they" were. Sometimes our parents felt like our jailers.

"So what do we do?"

I explained to her that she had to run to the shed first because she'd be in the least trouble if she got caught. Her mom would yell once and that would be it. I gave her the combination for the lock, told her to open it just enough to slip in, and then wait near the tire rack. I'd be right behind her when I was sure the coast was clear.

Bella nodded. She was fully on board with the adventure. My breath whooshed out as she ran. I wondered what she'd taste like. Lemon, like she smelled? Mint or something else like, bubble gum? Would she let me touch her breasts? Would I be able to slip my hand under her shirt? Would her skin be soft and smooth?

I looked right and left twice before I made my own run to the shed, opening the heavy door, slipping through, then pulling it closed behind me. It took a minute for my eyes to adjust to the dim light that came through the crack in the door and the dusty windows. Even when my eyes adjusted, Isabella was nowhere to be seen.

"Bella?" My heart sank with the idea that she'd gone home, too scared to meet me here.

I heard a scrape as the tire rack moved a bit. "Sorry. It could have been Mr. Perez or even Mama." Her own sigh was filled with relief.

"I thought you told me she was afraid of the spiders in here." It had been part of my plan when I eliminated who could possibly interrupt.

"She is, but if Mr. Wu needed something and no one else was here, I think she might try to come in."

I moved back toward the door and pushed it firmly shut, cutting out most of the light. There was enough, though. To see her clearly. The blood rushed down from my head again.

For the first time ever, I didn't hide my feelings from Isabella. Instead, I sucked up all my bravado and walked toward her until my chest was touching hers.

When she'd moved here, we'd been nearly the same height, but now I could see the top of her head. I willed her to look up, and she did. Tilting her head back, her eyes met mine, then immediately flickered down toward my lips.

That tiny movement knocked me for a loop. She wanted the same thing I did. She wanted me to kiss her. It wasn't all one-sided.

I don't know who moved, but in a moment, we were so close to each other that we were breathing the same dusty air.

Like I was at a stupid middle school dance, I fastened my hands behind her waist, pulling her that much closer. Slowly, so as not to scare her, I lowered my head until my forehead was nearly touching hers. I was so close to her mouth that I could practically taste her.

"What did you want to show me?" she asked, pulling away slightly.

I closed my own eyes and tilted my head back up. I stepped back, letting her go. Maybe I'd moved just a bit too fast. But we had time—not all the time in the world, but at least an hour before dinner was on the table. The whole "show her something" hadn't been a complete lie. When I'd been in here the other day, I'd heard the faintest scraping sound under the Chinese newspapers my parents never seemed to throw away.

I lifted the stack so she could see what was there.

"Mice? Rats?" I looked at her for confirmation. I don't think I'd ever seen either in Shanghai outside of an extermination store window.

Isabella leaned closer, her hair falling out of its loose ponytail, hiding her face so I couldn't read her feelings. She shrugged.

"Don't know."

Took me a second to remember we were talking about the little animals burrowed in the paper.

"Me either," I said. "I saw what I think was the mom running in and out from my bedroom window. When she had an entire apple in her mouth, I figured she must be feeding more than herself."

I was grateful to that rat. She'd given me the idea of taking Bella to the shed. If that mom had found enough privacy to have babies, there was enough for me to kiss Isabella.

"What's going to happen to them?"

I'd kind of wondered the same thing. "They'll grow up in a few weeks and move out into the woods, I guess. I don't know where they go for the winter." I didn't really care where they'd be next. They could stay here for all I cared. It was way more important to me that we'd kissed before the first snow set in. These little rodents would have to figure it out on their own.

Bella reached out a tentative finger toward the babies.

"Don't," I said taking hold of her hand again.

Her eyes locked with mine. "Why not?"

"I asked Mr. Potter about them." Mr. Potter was my Earth Science teacher at school. I'd wanted to make sure Bella wouldn't get rabies or tetanus if we came in here once I'd discovered the animals. "He said that New Jersey rodents carry all sorts of insects and diseases that could make us sick." That was only half true. If we were vaccinated, there was virtually no risk at all, Mr. Potter had said. But I didn't want Bella to be sidetracked by the furry creatures. That wasn't why I'd gone through all this trouble.

"Does that mean we should tell Mr. Perez to get rid of them?" she asked. Her tone said that exterminating them was a fate she wasn't interested in seeing, but she'd follow my lead because I was the son of the owner and her mother's boss. Once again, I wondered what had gone on in Philly or Camden or wherever she'd lived before. Sometimes I think she worried more about her mother's job than her mother did.

"I don't think so. It's not like we have any pets or farm animals here or anything. As long as we don't touch them, I think we should be okay."

I was disappointed when she dropped my hand, but my hope was renewed when she lifted the dust cloth from the red-and-gold-embossed velvet couch Min Li had stored in here. It was like Bella had read my mind.

I wasted no time in striding across the few feet between us and sitting as close to her as I dared without scaring her away. She walked her hand across the velvet cushion until it barely touched mine. I took the invitation and grabbed hers, rubbing my thumb along the skin that was softer than the couch.

I wanted to ask her to let me kiss her. Instead I said, "I'm glad you came to New Jersey." It was lame, but it was the best I could do. It was taking everything in my power not to lean into her, kiss her, push her down and slip my hand under her shirt. I pulled my eyes from where they'd drifted to her breasts and looked up. My knee fell toward hers. I could feel heat radiating from her skin, even with the cool air swirling around us.

"Me too," Bella said. She squeezed my hand, hard.

I took a deep breath, summoning the courage to speak. My "I like you, Bella" came out on a whoosh of air.

Her knee pressed harder against mine. My little semi boner went fully hard at that. She turned and looked at me. Then her hand came up, slipping into my hair, lifting it away from in front of my eyes.

In that moment, I knew she wanted me to kiss her as much as I wanted to. She was leaning in, shifting in tiny little increments. When her head tilted to the left, I tilted mine to the right. A whiff of strawberry hit my nose. Her lips were going to taste like fruit.

For a moment, panic seized me as I wondered if she'd been kissed before. Would I live up to some other Philly guy? Then she closed her eyes and her lips parted just enough for me to see her breath slip out, and desire replaced worry.

When I thought I was close enough to touch her, I only hit air.

She was up and off the couch and back behind the tires before I caught on. Then I heard it, the lift of the lock, the squeak of the hasp.

Fear killed my boner, and I ran to the door to head off

whoever was there. I unhooked the little lock I'd turned from the inside and pulled open the door a crack.

"Wu Jian, what are you doing in here?" It was Min Li, and that had been in English. Her decision not to use Mandarin told me that she already had a really good idea of what Isabella and I were doing in here.

I could tell from the look on Bella's face when she stepped out from behind the tire racks that she was hell-bent on saving me from Min Li's wrath.

That was probably the moment I knew that I loved her.

"I was showing Jake," she said, emphasizing my American name over my Chinese one. "I was showing Jake, uh, this rat that just gave birth." Then she ran over and lifted the very same papers I'd only shown her for the first time minutes ago. "They're mighty cute."

Min Li's eyes barely flickered over the tiny animals. She may not have given birth to me, but I knew her like a mother. Those rats or mice or whatever would be gone the minute Mr. Perez stepped foot on the property Monday morning. They didn't stand a chance.

"Wu Jian, this is not acceptable," Min Li said. This was in Mandarin.

"We're just looking at them. We didn't touch them or anything," I said, like that was the answer to her concern.

Her eyes narrowed. "You should not be out in this shed with this girl."

"Mother," I started, playing up to her. "We've been friends since she moved here."

"You're getting too old for these kinds of friendships."

"We only run in the woods and sometimes play games

together. She's taught me all the American card games."

"You've just turned sixteen years old. She's not quite your age, but not a child anymore, either. The last thing you want is for her to get pregnant and bind our two families together."

"I'm not...we're not...I wouldn't..." I was thinking about kissing her. That's all. The other... All of the other hadn't really crossed my mind, exactly.

Well, it had. It would be a lie to say it hadn't. I thought about doing that every morning and every night. But doing that required a willing participant. And Bella was too young. And even if she wanted to, and who's to say she would—

I stopped my thoughts and looked up to realize that I'd been quiet for too long.

"Do you understand what I'm saying?"

"I understand. I was just taking a little break before piano. I wanted to wait until Father was up." I little white lie. "He said I woke him the other day when I was practicing Beethoven's 'Piano Sonata twenty-three.'"

"Bah. He needs to put in the earplugs I bought him. Go do it now. Don't mind anything he says."

"Yes. Of course."

"Don't forget what I'm saying. This girl. Her mother is the help. Nothing more. They're lovely people, I'm sure. Your father would have not hired anyone unsuitable. But she will never be more than the daughter of the help.

"Your father and I have bigger plans for you. You may take over the business here in America one day when your father goes back to Shanghai. You'll definitely go to one of the top universities. You have a bright future that you must not trade for temporary enjoyment."

I stood mute again. This was the first time Min Li or Father had clued me in on their plans for me. I'd thought this whole America thing was temporary. That we could go back to China at any time. Now I knew they planned for me to attend university here. And take over Father's business. What did that mean? Make appliances? Make cars? Something else?

Suddenly, all that future responsibility sat heavy on my shoulders. I hadn't exactly thought about the future. Who did at my age? For fleeting moments, though, I thought I'd be able to chart my own path. Like maybe something else that wasn't in an office. I didn't quite know what yet.

Sometime while Min Li had been lecturing me, Isabella had been making the slow creep toward the door. She had one sneakered foot out the door when Min Li put a hand around her arm and stopped Bella in her tracks.

"Not yet," she said to Bella in clear, plain English.

"Do we have an understanding?" Min Li said to me, again in Mandarin.

I nodded. Embarrassed that there wasn't anything I could do to save Bella from Mother's wrath, I kept my head down and looked at my feet as I left the shed, trying to decide if I could get away with skipping Mandarin tonight. I'd make it up this weekend.

And Bella. I'd have to make it all up to her another time, because I didn't think Mother was right about her. In school, a teacher said America was different because anyone could be anything they wanted. I knew that wasn't the case in China, but maybe it could be true here not just for Isabella, but for me as well.

CHAPTER 9

NOW

"IS THIS IT?" Liling had draped herself across the red and gold couch Min Li had somehow moved in here. I think the relationship between my stepmother and me could be best described as tolerant. There was more make-believe between us than in all of Mr. Rogers' neighborhood. Every so often she's swoop in with Father and pretend that she loved me, did the mom act. I'd kiss her on the cheek and put up with the few minutes of intense scrutiny. Her last visit had yielded this couch. It was the first time I was grateful because it was a reminder of the good times Bella and I'd had.

Her gown lay across the fabric. She made the kind of picture photographers longed for. All pale skin with lace fanned out around her. The red lipstick on her mouth was an exact match for the couch. It just wasn't the picture in my mind. There was a huge disconnect between what was in front of me and what was in my mind's eye.

That picture was Bella, on the same red and gold couch

all those years ago in the shed. It wasn't that girl that I wanted, but the woman Isabella had become.

"Is what it?" I asked once I'd tuned back into the present. I thought I'd ditched her for the night, but somehow she'd followed me back to my apartment. After I'd left Bella, I'd come home ready to wind down, figure out what my strategy would be going forward. Before I could kick off a single shoe, my buzzer sounded and Liling was at the door. She wasn't going to let me shake her that easily.

She waved her hands around at the room. "Is this where you're living? There's hardly enough space to turn around."

I almost agreed with her out of habit. Agreed that eighteen hundred square feet and three bedrooms and three bathrooms was like living in a shack in the back of beyond in the hinterlands of China.

"I think this is big for most Americans. Most Chinese as well."

"Not anyone we know. I have a lot of space in the Malibu house. Daddy bought it for me while he builds something up the coast."

"It's convenient. I told you that. I have to be there tomorrow, early."

"I can't believe that guy pulled out his...his...on television. Will he lose his job?"

"We can't fire him from being a singer. Truth is, he'll probably be more rich and more famous after this."

"America is so weird. He won't lose face. His family won't be ostracized or anything. It's like you could do anything here."

Sometimes I almost felt like I *could* do anything, even if it wasn't always true. I fantasized that I could marry Isabella and no one would ask how we could love each other. We could have children and no one would treat them different for being half one thing and half another. The reality of pulling that off would be another thing entirely.

"I thought you were at the *Vanity Fair* after-party." Celebrity spotting used to be her thing.

"Boring. Same people at every damned party. Only this one had an extra helping of old creepers. Three different so-called producers tried to touch me. They didn't stop bothering me until I told them I was your girlfriend. Turns out they wanted green-lit television shows more than they wanted me."

"There are a few more after-parties. My assistant printed me a list. It's around here somewhere. Couldn't have lost it in a place this small."

"We could have our own party." Liling reached over and pulled a bottle of Louis XIII from somewhere under her skirt.

"Jesus, where did you get that?"

"Picked it up from the after-party downtown. No one will miss it."

"No one will miss an eight-thousand-dollar bottle of cognac?"

"They were a sponsor or something. There were bottles everywhere as decoration. Probably hoped we'd take them and Instagram ourselves holding them. I'm doing them a favor. Glasses?"

"Liling. I have an early meeting. We have to get together to figure out this Blue thing."

"It's Louis the thirteenth. You need a shot now. You'll be

fine in the morning as long as we don't drink the whole bottle. Remember that time we drank a whole bottle of Jägermeister?"

"We were so stupid back then. Do you remember where we got it?"

"My guess would be Cole's stash. Abbott was all about the snacks. Cole was all about the booze."

"Goddamn that was awful." It had been both Liling's and my first time being drunk. As we'd done years ago over the manga, we promised each other not to tell our parents about that one or about what had come after.

"I can't believe we survived that hangover," she said. "It was the worst of my life."

I stood up and walked over to the dining room. There were various stacks on the table where I should have been taking my meals. I shuffled through, ostensibly looking for after-party invitations or memos about avoiding curse words and genitalia on live television. But what I was really doing was hoping that Liling had forgotten about what had happened *after* the Jägermeister. Or at least would not mention it. It still made me cringe to think about it all these years later.

I found the stack and pulled a velvet envelope from it. Plucking the gold-embossed invitation from inside, my memory lined up with my immediate goal.

"There's a party in Bel Air at Drew O'Bryan's."

"Drew O'Bryan? He's out of rehab?"

"He's either in or out. Probably would be a party either way. I'm guessing he's out right now."

Lily couldn't help herself. I'd hoped that she couldn't.

She plucked the invitation from my hand with her perfectly manicured nails.

"This is a can't-miss party. Everybody will be so jealous if I Instagram this one."

"Should I call a car?"

My question was drowned out by a blast of music so loud, it set my teeth on edge. Nirvana filled my apartment. Not the words, but the insistent guitar riffs.

"Damn. That's loud! Reminds me of that band that girl used to like. The one who was the daughter of your house-keeper that you used to have a crush on, and they made you leave town for."

I tried to school my features. But I wasn't fast enough for Liling.

She walked close to me. Her front meeting mine. In her heels, we were eye to eye.

"What happened to her? Isabella was her name, right?"

She'd said that like she'd forgotten, but we both knew that she hadn't forgotten a single thing about Bella.

So many possible lies came to my lips. Not one came out, though. I was doing the complicated chess in my head of weighing telling Liling the truth and how exactly to keep that truth from becoming an issue for my father—or even worse, Min Li. I'd thought I'd done a good job yesterday of deflecting my father's questions. I wanted to keep the status quo.

While I was thinking, Liling was as well.

"Isabella Aconi worked at CBT in Philadelphia. She doesn't..."

Before I could catch her, Lily stalked across the small

apartment in her heels, the sound not audible above the music. But if I could have heard them, I'm sure the sound of the stilettos hitting wood was an angry staccato.

She jammed the O'Bryan invitation in her bag with one hand and extracted her phone with the other. At that point, I wished we were in China where Google and Facebook were banned. Where the extra step of logging on through a VPN may have slowed her down. But here in the middle of Los Angeles with all the openness in the world, there was little to stop her.

"Isabella Aconi. Vice President Program Practices at CBT. Los Angeles, California," she read. Probably from LinkedIn. "What's Program Practices?" Liling titled her head, narrowed her eyes.

"Network censor," I answered in English. The moments of beating around the bush were long past.

I could see her brain working. First through the translation. Then through the idea of it.

Balling her hand into a fist, Liling banged it on the adjoining wall. It didn't make a difference because another song started, its drum and guitar beat heavy and insistent.

"So if she's a vice president and a network censor, her job would have been to edit out Blue and his penis. But she didn't." Her mind chewed through the rest. "So she works across the street. Did you see her tonight?"

"She was there supervising a new girl."

"That didn't work out too well."

"I'm sure she'll have some ideas on how to get past this."

"At the meeting tomorrow that you need the huge night's sleep for?"

"It's her meeting at eleven."

"Goddam it, Wu Jian. Goddam it! Do you know, for one minute there I actually thought you'd bought the station for *me*. That you knew how much I wanted to tell stories and that you'd invested in the network so I could maybe produce that show I wrote the pilot for all those years ago when I was at Owen.

"But it's not about me. It's never in all these years been about me. You bought this for *her*. Maybe not *for* her, but so you could be near her. You know that other guys just call or text a woman, right? Buying an entire network is over-the-top cray cray.

"I've gotta go. Maybe this O'Bryan character will be interested in meeting me. Because guys are, you know…interested in me. I turn every one of them down. Every single one. But maybe I need to stop doing that."

"Maybe you do."

I could see that she was fighting back tears. The music was too damned loud. I banged on the wall myself this time for good measure.

"I don't mean…" I trailed off.

"But you do mean it. You've meant it every single time you've said it. I was so stupid for letting myself believe that you could change. For letting my mother and yours make me think if I just stuck around, and was nice enough or pretty enough or available enough, that you'd wake up one day and see me and fall in love with me for real. But you've never seen *me*. You've only ever seen *her*. I've been kidding myself for way too long and I think I'm done with that."

"Liling. Lily."

"Call me the car. Do whatever you have to do to get me out of here."

"I'm sorry."

"There's nothing to be sorry for. The truth has always been there at Woodward Tillman, before the engagement, after you gave me a ring, when you broke it off. This is just the first time we're speaking plainly is all."

I fished my phone from my pocket and walked out on the balcony. One call and there was a limo ready and waiting for Liling. Being in close proximity to the network had its perks, not all of them Isabella related.

"Good night, Wu Jian." She looked me directly in the eye. Her hands came up to caress my cheeks. I closed my eyes as she leaned in. The kiss was like the soft flutter of a moth, nothing more.

I could barely hear her "be safe" above the din of the neighbor's music.

"Maybe now I will be," I said.

Liling walked down the hall, gliding into the elevator that opened just as she'd pressed the button. She swept her dress from the closing door, disappearing behind the stainless steel.

Sadness filled me. Even though she wasn't what I wanted. What I needed. Liling had been such a fixture for so much of my life that I didn't know what it would be like without her.

That damned music. I slammed out of my apartment and went next door. I was done with this reminder of Isabella. I needed a break. At least until tomorrow, when I could work out the best way to approach the Blue issue, my dad, Min Li, Lily, and most importantly, Bella.

I knocked on number four twelve.

There was no response the first time, so I knocked again, this time with a lot more force. The abrupt halt to the music left a drum beat echo in my ears. Satisfied the other person had gotten the message, but was probably too embarrassed to come to the door, I started the walk back to my own. The noise of locks twisting made me look back.

I couldn't have been more shocked if someone had jammed a cattle prod up my ass when I saw the face peering out through the crack.

Bella.

For a long moment I stood stock-still, thinking that I'd somehow conjured her from my subconscious. That was ridiculous, though, so I looked again to make sure. It was Isabella alright.

I turned on my heel and stuck my leather-clad foot in the door before she could slam it.

She was as surprised as I, but like the girl I'd known in Jersey, she rallied quickly.

"Are you stalking me?" It took me a full second to place the word. She thought I was following her. It was both so right and so wrong at the same time. "I hate to bring you up to speed on American labor laws," she was saying, "but working for CBT doesn't mean I'm a slave or indentured servant or something. The minute I walked off the lot, I was off the clock. No locking me in the building or anything."

I hated that a few labor rights abuses in China had tainted our relationships in America. It would be up to me to prove to the employees at CBT that we were going to be good and fair business owners. I added that to the mental list of things I'd need to do to make this endeavor succeed. Because if I knew one thing, it was that failure wasn't an option.

It was rude, but I couldn't help it when my eyes traveled from the top of Bella's beautifully messy hair to her bare toes. Though I knew better, had been raised to value modesty, I couldn't help but look at the place where her robe had fallen open. Where I could see the swell of a breast I hadn't touched in so many years, but that I yearned to reach forward and caress now.

"Bella," slipped from my lips like a hiss. Sometimes I thought there was no single cure for this obsession other than possessing the woman herself.

"Isabella," she said, her tone snapping me from the reverie of memories of the times in our past when we'd been in sync.

"Isabella, then. This is fortuitous." Luck was prized in Chinese culture. I'd laughed in the face of and abandoned a lot of superstitions, but the importance of luck wasn't one of them.

"Four syllables. Your father's tuition to Woodward Tillman Hall didn't go to waste after all," Isabella snapped.

There were so many issues between us, my being shipped off to private boarding school being one of them. I hadn't planned this at all, but I pushed my foot farther into the door. Maybe one by one, we could conquer them.

"Are you going to invite me in?"

She pulled her robe even tighter, hiding herself from me. "I'm indisposed at the moment."

"We lived together for six, nearly seven years. I've seen it all."

I schooled my mind not to jump back to all the pieces I'd seen of her, which allowed me to put them together like a puzzle in my mind, creating one whole nude Isabella.

She stepped back and I took that as an invitation of sorts. It wasn't an outright denial at least. Isabella was in such a hurry to slam the door behind me that she nearly caught my suit jacket.

"Watch it. Mom had this tailored," I warned. It was stupid but I wanted her to see me.

"Singapore," she retorted.

"I feel like I ought to give you a prize." She'd learned more from Min Li than she'd probably admit, even if those lessons had been offered couched in insults and put-downs.

"If you're here to talk about your stupid office thing, I'm happy to let you know that suitable accommodations equal to your contribution to our department will be made."

Keeping up with Isabella these days was a challenge. It was a far cry from the days when I could practically read her mind, and she could read mine.

"I was here about the music," I said.

"Revival? I know you didn't have Google in China, but now that you're here, I'm sure you're resourceful enough to figure out how to get whatever information you need about the band," she said, her hand still holding her robe together with a death grip.

"Not that music," I started. "I came by to ask you to turn down *yours*."

She rolled her eyes. "None of the actual residents have ever complained."

I'm sure that Mafia princess persona had kept them quiet out of fear of bodily harm.

"That's not true." I look her in the eye, willing her to see me *now*, and past the me who'd been less than I should have been with her. "Your newest neighbor is lodging a complaint."

I walked farther into her apartment that was as generically upscale as my own. It was one of those places that tried to create a feeling of wealth and home, but achieved neither. I unbuttoned my jacket, able to relax for the first time in hours, and took a seat on her ottoman. I'd forgotten that Isabella could make anyplace feel like home.

"I haven't met him...or her," Bella said, her eyebrows pulling together in question.

"But you have." I held out my hand and she took it absently, her manners winning out over her aversion to my overtures. "Jake Wu. I'm in four ten."

She tried to pull away from my grip. I'd held on too long for it to be considered polite.

"Four ten," she parroted. She pulled her hand away and shook it like she needed to get the feeling back. It was the opposite of what was going on in my fingers, where all of my feeling seemed to have concentrated in my digits. Her "if you'll excuse me" was tossed over her shoulder as she ran up the few stairs to what I assumed was her carbon-copy master bedroom and bath.

I took off my jacket. It was a bit warm. Then I stood and made my way through her downstairs. It was hardly personalized. Or it was personalized in a copy of a furniture store catalog. I recognized some minor local artists, the Scandinavian furniture that was in equal parts expensive and uncomfortable, and the hand-loomed rugs. Even if it didn't look like how I'd imagined her place to be, it smelled like Isabella, a mix of her and a perfume that was unfamiliar. It was far more subtle than what she'd worn twenty years ago, but I could smell it in the fabric nonetheless.

The kitchen didn't look lived in. That was different. Both Min Li's kitchen, where her mother, Maria, had cooked, and their kitchen in the guesthouse were always laden with the smells of onion and garlic. This room had granite and wood and tile and, like mine, was absent of smell.

The fridge held a couple of salads, open wine bottles— white and red—and some kind of flavored creamer. I don't know what she ate or where she ate, but it wasn't here.

I expected frozen dinners in the freezer, but there was only alcohol. A couple of flavored vodkas lay on their side. A third bottle with an unfamiliar label had me reaching my hand in and bringing it out for a closer look.

Gin.

I unscrewed the cap and the telltale smell of pine wafted from the ice-cold bottle. I turned it to read the label. Not just gin, but Dutch gin.

Daniel.

I'd known it in my bones when Isabella had waved that Blackberry around. He still had a hold of her. All these years later, she was still beholden to Daniel. Not for the first time, I wondered what in the hell he'd done to have this hold on Isabella for her entire adulthood so far.

She'd shed me faster than a snake molts its skin. But Daniel, he clung like a barnacle to a ship.

Closing the freezer door, I plunked the thick glass bottle on the counter. I found a highball glass in one of the cabinets and poured myself a couple of fingers and went back to the beautifully uncomfortable living room. Between Daniel and Blue and Lily, I sorely needed it.

Isabella came in, her hair slicked back, dressed like she was going to practice kick boxing at the gym. I held out the cut glass in a mock toast.

"Top-shelf stuff, this." I took my third or fourth sip. The cold liquid went down smooth, warming me from the inside out. I wanted to stay like this forever, in companionable silence. Maybe not forever, because there was so much more I wanted from her, but for the foreseeable future. But if I'd learned anything about life, it was that it did not remain static no matter how much I'd wanted that at different times in the past.

She nodded in acknowledgement and got herself a glass of the strong spirit. Isabella took one sip, then another. I saw her shoulders drop and a breath escape her lungs as the alcohol hit her.

"Why are you really here, Jake?"

"The neighbor thing was an accident, I swear," I said. That was true. The answer to the bigger question, I didn't quite know how to answer.

She shrugged.

"Your family likes nice things. There aren't but a handful of these kinds of apartments in the city. You picked the one closest to the network. Makes sense."

"You always did like your music loud," I said. It was one of dozens of things I remembered about her. Father had not been a fan. He'd tolerated it when Min Li wasn't there. I'm not sure what happened when Mother was in town, but Isabella all but disappeared during those times, especially after the incident in the shed.

"I can't feel it unless I *feel* it." She stamped her foot for emphasis. I envied her that ability to feel something so deep down in her bones. To be moved by it.

"You loved that Led Zeppelin concert. I still can't believe our parents let us go by ourselves." I wanted to kick myself for not thinking before I spoke. For not censoring memories of one of the best and worst nights of our lives. "Unless..." I trailed off. Regret could not make my last words unsaid. I'd have to be so much more careful about the minefields between us.

"Yeah, unless they wanted us out of the way for a night," she said baldly.

I took a gulp of the cold gin. It did not help me with my parched throat. I cast my eyes about, looking for something to latch on to that we could share that wasn't tainted by the past.

"I never pictured you in a place like this," I said. Her mother had always made their house cozy with squishy couches and fluffy pillows. I'd only been in there a few times, and not for long, but it had always felt more like home than my own house, with its formal furniture and clashing prints.

"Where did you see me ending up, Jake? Because I didn't plan to take your mother's advice and work as someone's servant."

God, why did it seem like she took everything the wrong way, that she was always ready to misunderstand what was said?

I backtracked as quickly as I could.

"Of course not. You have to forgive her traditional ideas. You have to forgive your own mom," I said. It wasn't that I wanted everyone to hold hands and sing "Kumbaya." It wasn't that I'd been in California one time too many. It was that I wanted to move on. I wanted all of us to move on. There was nothing, not a thing I could do about the past. I didn't see a reason our future couldn't be different.

Isabella's screwed-up features told me she wasn't on the same page, though.

"I don't have to forgive her anything."

"You don't think?" I'd done my best to forgive Father. He'd admitted that women were his weakness. If he hadn't had that exact weakness, I wouldn't exist. It was a character flaw, but by no means fatal. He hadn't really hurt anyone with his infidelities. Min Li had signed on knowing full well who he was. And as far as I could tell, she was the truly aggrieved party, if there was one at all.

"I'm not my mother. She's an adult. She was an adult long before me. I have no control over what she does."

"Why can't you try?" It's not that I thought we could be one big happy family. That ship had probably sailed, landed in China, and had never come back. What I wanted was for there to be less hate and less animosity all around. It would make it easier for us if everyone got along. Easier for us to be together if she weren't still like a dog gnawing over that old bone of the past.

"If this is why you're still here, you can leave," she said. Isabella's headshake was slow and defeated. "I've let you stay this long because we did know each other once. We were friends once. But if this is going to devolve into our parents' shit, I'm out. I got out when I went to Owen. Washed my hands of it. Put it behind me. Whatever other clichés you can think of."

I'd tried my best to keep it at bay, but anger and jealousy rose from deep inside me. Came out roaring like a lion.

"Who's paying for this apartment?"

"My finances aren't your concern."

I was signing her checks. In a sense, her finances were very much my concern. I knew better than to say that. Instead, I got to the meat of what I wanted to know. "That was Daniel calling, right?" I hefted my glass so the recessed lighting glinted off the surface. "Dutch liquor. Seven-thousand-dollar-a-month apartment. Doesn't take Agatha Christie—"

She slammed down her drink. Gin beaded and rolled across the wood table. She stood stock-straight. "That's it. Get your jacket."

"Why?"

"Because I'm an adult. I'm not dependent on you or your dad anymore."

"Aren't you?" I think I felt as defeated as she looked. I wanted things to change. But they hadn't. Isabella wasn't her own woman, she was still an object of Daniel's, to do with what he will.

"There are other networks. More than there ever were. I can keep tits and ass off one channel as well as I've done it on CBT. The Wus no longer control me. I'm not Maria Sofia. I'll *never* be like her."

Wow. She couldn't see it. She wasn't ready.

I wasn't sure what needed to happen. As long as she had no problem relying on Daniel, though, I wasn't sure I could trust her feelings. I needed space. I hadn't been ready to confront her, convince her, but this neighborly chat had been too enticing to refuse. I should have let her shut the door when she'd wanted to.

"You're exactly like her, Bella. Trading your body for a house, money, designer stuff."

The sting of her palm against my face was a surprise. I looked at her, down at myself. This was a thousand miles from where I wanted to be with her. Deep down I knew I wasn't angry with her. I was resentful over Min Li's lies, her intent on continuing to deceive the world to save face. Angry as hell at Father for lying to me, wrapping Maria Aconi into his web of deceit. Angry at myself for not doing something earlier, for not getting out from under their thumb. Angry at Isabella for not seeing her worth, for still relying on Daniel. All of it burned a hole in my chest the size of my heart.

Something had gone terribly wrong in the last few minutes, or maybe the last twenty years, I couldn't decide which. I wasn't a hundred percent sure there was anything to salvage not until something changed, but I didn't know what.

I needed to get back to my little place next door and think about my next step.

I turned and let myself out.

CHAPTER 10

"DAMNED KIDS from Jersey clogging up the city. If they closed the bridges and tunnels, we'd all be a lot better off."

"They're like the rats that are taking over the city. There are more of them every time you turn around."

I looked over my shoulder to see two white guys laughing. They were like twenty-five-year-old versions of Evan and Cole. Perfect haircuts, perfect clothes, and the confidence of knowing that the world was made for them.

All the while, I was what they called a fish out of water. I'd just learned that phrase last week in school and thought it described exactly what it was like to be here. I was forever trying to make my way back to the ocean. I think my ocean was China. But Father was committed to this place while he tried to change the course of Grandfather's business legacy. He was convinced that China would go from poor to rich as Chinese products took over store shelves.

I didn't think anyone wanted anything from China,

really. Maybe Chinese food. Weird Americanized versions were available in nearly every strip mall. But no one wanted our stuff here any more than those privileged boys in Penn Station wanted us kids from Jersey invading New York City.

It didn't matter what those two or anyone else thought. I was here with Isabella without any parental supervision.

I grabbed her hand and pulled her away from the crowd the minute we got off the escalator.

Like we'd done a hundred times since she'd moved in, I bowed my forehead toward hers conspiratorially. "Bridge," I whispered.

Her smile told me she got it. That some people may not like us, but it didn't matter, none of it mattered as long as we liked each other.

"Tunnel," she said.

Then we laughed like hyenas for a long time. Hyenas, that was another one I'd learned this year. I had no idea what a hyena was or whether it laughed. I didn't think animals *could* laugh.

Isabella asked me the question she'd been asking over and over all the way to Manhattan from New Jersey.

"How did you do it?"

I shrugged. There were no magical powers I could point to. Father was like that, capricious. One moment he was as strict as Min Li, in the next he'd allow me to skip lessons or watch prohibited movies or play video games. It was a guy thing, I think. He hadn't quite forgotten what it was like to be a boy and want to do more than study or be loyal to family.

A couple of months ago, I'd taken a deep breath, braced myself, then walked into his office and asked if I could take

Isabella to Led Zeppelin, extra emphasis on her mom not allowing Isabella to go on account of the fast girls in Toms River.

"Maria...Ms. Aconi, will let Isabella go to Manhattan and see a concert if I can go with her."

"What kind of concert?"

"A band called Led Zeppelin. Rock and roll."

He nodded. "Something totally American, that rock and roll."

"So...can we go?"

"When is it?"

"The Saturday after Thanksgiving."

"Min Li says that all the stores put up their Christmas decorations then. You should go look at those."

I tried to hide my complete shock and Father's uncharacteristic joviality. Maybe the cooler weather had changed his disposition. People talked about how much they loved summer here. But once I could smell burning wood and see smoke curling from chimneys, everyone seemed like they were in a nicer mood.

"Stop giving me that face. I was young once. If you're going to take over this business in America someday, then you'll need to be familiar with their culture. You can't get that from Mandarin lessons and playing the piano. You get other things from that, but not everything that you need.

"When you go to meetings, they're going to want to shake your hand and ask you about sports, or movies, or television. The men who do business here want to talk about more than business. Same as in China, but different."

I nodded like he was reciting Tang Dynasty poetry.

"I'll arrange the tickets and some pocket money. I'll talk to Maria. I think she's too strict with that girl sometimes. She's a good student, right, Isabella?"

"Sure," I said. Then nodded my head in emphasis. I had zero idea if Isabella did well in school. I knew that education was important to Maria, and Isabella complained about all the homework talk from her mom. But I didn't know much more than that. I crossed my fingers and hoped she at least had a "B" average and, if she didn't, that Father would always be none the wiser.

"She and Min Li have that in common. I'll get both of them on board with this, if not with giving you guys a little bit of a break."

"Father." I wanted to fall to my knees in gratitude, but resisted. "Thank you."

"Thank me by working on your piano."

I'd nodded, cracked my fingers, and then had gotten to work on the concerto I was supposed to perform at a winter recital in December.

I looked at Isabella, and I got that feeling low in my stomach, like something was twisting in my gut, but in a good way. As if by some tacit agreement, our hands never lost contact. If anyone had asked, I'd have said that I'd been charged with making sure I didn't lose my housekeeper's daughter in the big city. But the truth of the matter was that I wanted to touch her.

Since that day in the shed, my need for her had only grown stronger. But Min Li had been much more vigilant in the last few weeks. Whenever she saw Isabella and me together, she was quick to find a task Isabella needed to ask her mother to do or studies I needed to attend to. Now that we were alone, though, truly alone for the first time in a long time, I wanted to be near her, near enough that I could smell the scent of her perfume, her shampoo, her lip gloss.

I wanted to be her first kiss, her first everything.

Isabella hesitated a long moment.

"I hope you like it," she said. She looked so uncertain, all I wanted to do was pull her in for a hug and reassure her that she could do nothing wrong. That the night was already perfect.

She was quiet so long that I jiggled her hand to bring her back to me.

"You okay?"

"Sorry." Even though she was standing right here in front of me, I could see that Isabella's mind was far away elsewhere.

"You still want to do this?" I asked, tilting my head toward the thousands of people pushing their way toward Madison Square Garden. "We don't have to. It's New York. Dad gave me a few hundred dollars. We could do anything."

I really meant that.

Anything.

I'd be happy doing anything or nothing with Isabella. Looking at all those dressed-up department store windows. Eating a dessert from any one of the cultures represented by all the restaurants we were passing. Or we could even go to Rockefeller Center. On the news, they'd said it was the biggest tree ever, thirty meters. I'd take her to look at the lights and even try ice skating if she was daring, hot chocolate if she wasn't.

"I really have to go to this."

"Why Led Zeppelin?" I asked. She didn't answer while we navigated the escalators and stairs that finally got us to our seats.

"My dad," she said as she pocketed her mittens and pushed her coat into the seat. "Led Zeppelin was my dad's favorite band. Every Saturday, he'd wake us up by blasting one of their songs. Then Arturo and I would come downstairs and dance until Mama had breakfast ready."

"Sounds fun."

"Your mother would never do anything like that. Your father either. But my parents were like that...back then. Totally fun. Kind of lame, but fun, too. I really wanted to go so that when I see my dad again, I can tell him about this. About how I'd seen his favorite band ever right here in New York. If he were here, he'd totally have taken my brother and me."

"He's in Italy?"

"Yeah. He went back after the divorce."

"Why did he go so far away?"

"Mama said it's because he's a mama's boy who doesn't know how to live on his own. To be honest, I'm not sure. It's weird, but no one will tell me anything. It's like they think I'm a kid who can't understand. I mean, I get it. They stopped loving each other for some reason and split up. Lots of other parents do it."

I took off my own coat, but remained silent. Given the true mystery of my own parentage, I kind of felt like maybe they were keeping her in the dark on purpose. There was probably more—a lot more—they weren't telling her. But I didn't want to be the bearer of possibly bad news. Instead, I grabbed her hand and twirled her around.

"Hey!" she gasped. "There's no music yet."

"Doesn't matter. We should dance anyway. I've never gotten to dance with you."

"You didn't go to any of the school dances when we were in the same school. Your father would have let you go," she said, with emphasis on that second to last word.

"Maybe. But I didn't want to go if you couldn't."

"Maria Sofia Aconi would have me in a convent if she thought she could get away with it."

"She isn't that bad. She just loves you. Wants to keep you away from all the boys who'd jump your bones given half a chance."

"Nobody likes me."

"The boys talk about you."

"What do they say?"

"That you're cute, but they're afraid of your father."

"Right...Shorty Aconi. It worked on Evan and Cole. It worked a little too well, huh?"

I looked at the stage, where a bustle of activity had started. I thought her little Mafia princess act had worked perfectly. The guys all stayed away from her, leaving the path clear for me.

She was bouncing in her seat. I took my hand and steadied her jiggling knee, steadying *her*. I wanted to kiss her so bad. Right now seemed like the perfect time.

Picking up her hand, I started to tell her what I was

feeling when a group of people our parents' ages scooted by, stepping on both our feet. They looked like they'd had a lot of drinks before they'd come down to their seats.

When the lights dimmed and then spotlights swooped through the arena, I knew I'd lost my chance.

I didn't know if I'd ever grow to love American rock music, but I loved Led Zeppelin. I loved that they brought a smile to Isabella's face, a sway to her arms, a swing to her hips. She sang along, screaming her heart out beside people three times her age who'd probably actually grown up with this music on the radio.

The chords of their last song filled the air, then disappeared in the screams of everyone there. They left the stage and it looked like they weren't coming back. I turned then to look at Isabella, trying to transmit all I couldn't say with my eyes.

Something akin to electric shock winged its way through my body, and I knew in that second that she got it. Got what I felt—and she returned the feeling.

We followed the crush of people out, but what had been a crowd as thick as a flock of birds thinned out within minutes. Thousands of people turned to a handful.

"Can we get that dessert?" Isabella asked.

I'd never seen her eat much of the cakes her mom made for my father, but I think, like me, she didn't want the night to end.

"Let's walk a little first. I want to show you something." I led her around the corner until we were on Thirty-fourth Street. Her gasp told me I'd made the right decision.

"It's so pretty!" she said, looking through the department store windows at the elaborate holiday designs. Little animatronic Santas and elves and angels frolicked in what looked like real snow. She stared at all the little scenarios for nearly half an hour before I encouraged her to have a walk past the Empire State Building, which was also lit for the holidays. Around another corner, we found a little Greek diner.

They treated us like we were adults, asking how many were in our party and whether or not we wanted dinner or just coffee.

"Dessert," I answered.

"Menu's on the back," the waitress said. "No more key lime pie, but we've got cherry, Boston cream, and lots of pumpkin."

"I'll have pumpkin," Isabella announced. "And a hot chocolate, please."

"You, sir?"

"Cherry."

"To drink?"

I waffled between hot chocolate and coffee. Neither seemed palatable. "Tea, please."

"Coming right up."

"So? What did you think? Wasn't that the best concert ever?" Isabella enthused.

"It was good."

"That last song was my dad's favorite. I think it's a sign from God that he's thinking of me."

"Right. I hope so." I didn't want to talk about parents. I have to admit I was the tiniest bit jealous that she'd had such a close relationship to her father. Sounded like the stuff of all the American television shows, with the goofy guy who makes a lot of mistakes, serves pizza and ice cream when the mom's away, but shows lots of love and affection for the kids. Love from my own family came in the form of rules and obligation.

I ate the too-sweet gooey pie and shook off the feeling of melancholy that was threatening to descend over me. Tonight, at least, we were free of all that. It was just the two of us in the biggest city in America. We could do anything.

"Here's your check. No hurry. It's looking brutal out there. Let me know if you want a refill on your drinks." The waitress dropped a small piece of pale blue lined paper on the table. Like my father had taught me, I left double the ten-dollar tab.

"Ready?"

Isabella nodded and pulled on her coat and mittens. I could see what the waitress was talking about the moment we stepped outside. A fog had come down that made it impossible to see the difference between buildings. Street and neon lights melted into a blur.

"Want to go anywhere else?" I asked, at a loss.

She peered back into the diner. "It's twelve thirty."

I did a quick calculation in my head. "We should probably head back. Father didn't say anything about a...what do you call it...a time we should be home?"

"A curfew?"

I nodded and committed that missing word to memory. "No need to get them mad."

"They may never let us do this again if we get them mad."

"I'd very much like to do this again." I rested my forehead against Isabella's. Even in the fog, I could see our breaths mingling. I tried to move my head one way, changing the angle, moving our lips closer together, but it didn't quite work. I couldn't quite kiss Isabella.

"Is Penn Station that way?" She pointed. Reluctantly, I steered us both back toward the massive train station, then around to Port Authority.

The posted timetable indicated it was going to be a very long ride. As if reading my mind, Isabella said, "C'mon. It won't be so bad. At least we can entertain each other."

Isabella was the opposite of entertaining on the bus. Brooding and gloomy was more like it during the first half hour. Now she was sleeping quietly.

Her mood had been all over the place today. I'd thought she'd wanted to kiss me. But maybe it was one hundred percent on my end. My wanting to be with her clouding my judgment as to what she wanted. After listening to guys talk, it wouldn't be the first time.

Turned out none of us could read girls. I'd always thought girls wanted what we did, but maybe my father was right, and we were different creatures altogether. Us with our needs and girls with whatever it was they wanted, like cooking and cleaning and making sure everyone was doing what they were supposed to do.

My hands were shaking with the urge to reach out and touch her. Maybe I needed to wait for a sign. I interlaced my cold fingers and jammed them between my knees. I didn't want to be that horny guy who didn't get it right. I'd wait for my chance.

"Jake?" Isabella's voice quavered with that one-word question.

I turned toward her, not lifting my head from the rest behind me. "You're not asleep? It's after one."

Isabella's face was a frown of confusion. "I..." she started. Then she shifted, her movements suddenly deliberate. The armrest between us was shoved up and in less than a second, her hand grabbed at both of mine.

My pulse suddenly slowed at the inevitability of it all. Then it sped up like it was a bomb ticking toward detonation.

She leaned closer. I leaned closer. I could feel the hair on my forehead shifting with her every breath.

"Oh, Bella," I huffed, my secret endearment for her escaping before I had a chance to edit myself.

"Why do you call me that?"

"It means beautiful," I disclosed. She was the most beautiful girl in the world to me. I could stare at her all day long and never get tired.

"Do you think—"

I cut her off before she could spiral into teenage girl insecurity.

"That you're the most beautiful girl I've ever known? Yes, Bella. Yes."

She leaned just that tiny bit toward me, telling me without words that she was ready, that it was time for what I'd been waiting for all night, waiting for all year.

I took her smooth jaw in my hand and leaned in, putting my lips on hers as lightly as possible.

Min Li was constantly yelling at Isabella and me when we were outside running around on those days when dark clouds loomed overhead. This briefest of touches. This is what I imagined that being struck by lightning was like. The bolt of electricity that shot through me was so powerful, I thought my hair might stand on end.

Gasping, I pulled back. It was nearly too much, that touch.

While I thought about how I should approach kissing her again, Bella took over. This time she leaned in and pressed her lips against mine, hard.

I couldn't stop myself then. Pressing toward her, I slipped my hand from her jaw, past the soft, warm shell of her ear, and into the silk of her hair. Gripping hard, I pulled her ever closer. Bella's hands mimicked mine, and her fingers sent goose bumps through my scalp. I slanted my mouth, urging her to open to me, thrusting my tongue inside, rubbing against hers.

Once I started, the boner stirring in my pants made it so I couldn't stop. I barely caught a breath as I kissed her once, then again and again, until we were close to our stop, until the bus slowed and crunched gravel into the commuter parking lot.

"Let's get a cab," I said as I kept our hands joined and pulled her toward the first in line of the three cabs idling at the curb, the smoke from their tailpipes leaving acrid-smelling trails.

"Who's going first?" the cabbie threw back at us.

"Same address," I said.

He shook his head and tsked under his breath. Normally,

I was worried about condemnation from Americans. It usually meant I'd made some kind of crass cultural mistake. With Isabella's hand in mine, her warm body pressing against my side, his opinion held no sway. Faster than I expected, we were at the end of the driveway on Freehold Road.

"Want me to drive up?"

"Might wake our parents. Here is fine," I said. The cabbie's huff was even bigger this time. America was nothing like China, though. There was little need to explain to anyone how we lived our life. What they thought couldn't hurt us.

We were still holding hands when we watched the red taillights disappear into the nighttime mist.

"Are you tired?" Bella asked. With longing, I watched the breath escape her lips.

"Not the least bit." I searched my head for a way that I could prolong this night I didn't want to end. "You want to watch a movie?"

"What movie?" she asked.

I blinked once, then again. Which movie? I turned my eyes toward hers and smiled big. More than once, that had been enough, like when we were with her mother or my father, for her to get the message without words. Telepathically, I told her that I had zero care about which movie. What I wanted to do was be in our den, the bright wallpaper obscured by the darkness, and kissing her in the flickering light of the television. I needed that blue light to see her when I kissed her, when I lifted her shirt and maybe undid her bra.

When I shifted, she nodded, and I knew she got it.

"I would very much like to watch a movie with you, Jake Wu. Where?"

I pulled her toward me and kissed her again. To hell with where. We could stand out here all night for all I cared. I fitted my hand to her face and slanted my mouth against hers again. Bella laid her free hand against my chest and pushed gently.

"Shit. I forgot my mittens on the bus."

"I'll keep you warm, don't worry." I'd been so busy trying to get closer to her, that I'd forgotten it was cold and damp outside. I weighed the best place we could be together.

"Your house? You said your mother sleeps like a rock. My house won't work because Dad gets up in the middle of the night half the time to make calls to China. I've seen him stick his head in any room with a light on, on the way down to his office."

Isabella nodded. I could see her weighing the same pros and cons in her own head. "The guest room," she concluded. I let her lead me up the driveway toward the guesthouse.

I didn't remember any kind of TV in the room, nor a VHS player, but that didn't matter. I knew there was a comfortable bed in there. We could hang out there. My brain was on overload with the thought of lying with her. I watched her turn her own key in the door lock. In a moment we were in. She pushed the door closed much too loudly.

"Shhhh." I put my fingers to my lips.

"Your shush is too loud," she whisper-shouted.

We both laughed at that, then the whole shushing sequence started again.

We were walking down the short hall when I nearly

bumped her. She'd come to an abrupt halt. When our eyes met, hers were filled with something that looked like fear. Immediately, I backed up a step.

"I only want to kiss you, Bella," I reassured her. "Hold you for a while before I go back to my house." It wasn't true, exactly. But I was willing to let her take the lead. I was older than her and needed to remember that.

We tiptoed the remaining steps, though Isabella faced me the whole time. Her eyes did little to hide the fear and want battling within her. When we got inside, with the door firmly closed against her mother's possible hearing, I'd tell her that it was the same for me. That I too wanted more, but didn't have a clue about how to go about it. That I thought it would be best if we could figure it out together.

She reached behind her back and turned the knob, pushing into the room. I followed her as closely as I dared without making us both trip. We bumped into each other anyway, which set Isabella to giggling. I was about to shush her again when she reached into the room and flicked on a switch. She never turned around, instead wrapping her arms around my neck.

Movement caught the corner of my eye. I blinked to make sure there wasn't any trick of the light, but there wasn't.

Father's bare ass was in the air.

As hard as I could, I shoved Isabella away from me. What I was seeing didn't...couldn't exist in the same universe as Bella and me.

"Father," I snapped.

When Isabella's confused eyes landed on me, I realized

I'd switched to Mandarin. That didn't matter at all. She didn't need to understand. I wanted to push her out of the room. Save her from my father's bad behavior. The way he'd been moving before I'd walked in the door, I knew he'd been doing what *I'd* wanted to be doing. But it was wrong. Wrong that I was seeing him lying on someone and grunting like a pig.

"Get out, Wu Jian, this is none of your business."

"What are you doing?"

"It's obvious. I need you to leave, and take that girl with you. She shouldn't see this."

"Why are you here? We have our own house." Not that I wanted to know that he was having an affair. But if it had happened with my real mother, and Min Li was forever out of town, it followed that he'd get his needs met. "Or hotels. I was just in New York. There are lots of hotels there. I'm old enough that you could have left me alone."

My father moved from lying on top of the woman and shifted to the side. She pulled a blanket and sheet up to her chin while Father wrapped himself in the dark red and dark blue duvet. I looked from my father, only to see Isabella's mother next to him.

He was fucking my girlfriend's *mother*?

My head filled with the kind of static that came at the end of a home movie when the tape ran out.

Maria's voice cut right through that static. "Isabella Beatrice. What in heaven's name do you think you're doing?"

Isabella whipped around. She'd kept her head buried in her hands when she'd assumed it was my father and some anonymous woman like I had. She was only slightly more stunned than when I'd pushed her. I was so sorry for that. I'd only wanted to spare her the embarrassment of Father seeing us kissing or her seeing Father. But this was so very much worse.

"Mama?" Isabella asked, as if she couldn't believe her eyes. I understood how she felt, as I could hardly believe my own.

"How many times have I told you, Isabella, that boys only want one thing? You promised me that you'd stay a virgin as long as you were under my roof."

This was news to me. My jaw opened, then shut. What could I say? I'd have gone as far as she'd wanted.

"I wasn't going to sleep with Jake, Mama," she answered. But her voice was small and wavered between the truth and what her mother wanted to hear.

"Then what were you doing with that boy coming into this room?"

I was working through what I could say in English that could help when Isabella spoke again.

"What about Daddy?"

It took me a long moment of translation and processing to realize that she wasn't talking about Father, but her own father, the one her mother had divorced a while ago.

Maria snorted like Isabella had cursed.

"Francis Aconi? Don't you ever speak that man's name in my house again."

"He's my daddy, Mama! When he's done being mad at you, I'm sure he's going to come back for me. Take me to

Disney World like he promised. Maybe I'll even get to spend the summer in Italy with him and Arturo."

Other than earlier tonight, this was the most I'd heard her talk about her old family in Philadelphia. I'd wondered, but hadn't wanted to pressure her. I'd had my own family secrets. In America, it seemed that confidences were to be traded, and I hadn't wanted to make that exchange.

"Get your head out of the clouds, Izzie. Francis Aconi isn't any kind of father," Maria said. Her voice reminded me of Min Li's in that it held no maternal kindness.

"Daddy *is* my father, Mama. I know you divorced him or he divorced you or whatever, but he'll always be my father."

"Izzie—he was never your father." Maria's voice was laced with resignation. "Francis Aconi isn't your flesh-and-blood father. When he figured that out, he was on the first plane to Gallipoli so he could sit at his mother's knee and bitch about me. That man never took responsibility for one damned thing."

"He's not...my dad?"

"Never was. And you can stop all that talk about Disney or whatever, because Francis Aconi is never coming back."

The whole time Maria and Isabella had been arguing, Father had been pulling on his clothes. He'd been inching toward the door in his weekend tracksuit, so he was standing next to me when Maria had said the last.

I wanted to comfort Isabella, but that would have to come later. Now wasn't the time.

I was about to follow my father out this door, down the hall, and out the other door when time seemed to come to a complete standstill. Bella let out a big hiccup—then she was doubled over, and all of the Manhattan diner food came up on the floor.

I *did* follow Father out then. Neither one of us said a thing as we walked to the main house. I went to my room and he to his. I sat down at my desk and shook my head.

My mother wasn't my mother. Her father wasn't her father. It was a hell of a thing that we had in common.

CHAPTER 11

NOW

WHATEVER ISABELLA HAD GOING ON HERE WAS worthy of an Oscar. I looked around the room. Maybe not an Oscar, but at least a Golden Globe.

The room was lit just so. I strode in ready to take my seat at the head of the table, but Isabella was already in it, lifted up so that she would be half a head taller than anyone else who took a seat. I maneuvered to the other end of the table. It was still a power position from which I could keep my eyes on Bella.

The rest of the executives filed in one by one, taking seats around the table. It was going to be a full house. My own assistant, who I hadn't thought to contact, rolled back in a seat behind mine. She was good at anticipating my needs like that. She definitely earned points for that one.

Once everyone was done shifting, Bella cleared her throat.

"Gentlemen." Oh so effectively, she paused. Even though

they'd probably deny it, each of the men shifted a millimeter forward in their seats, anticipation tightening their jaws.

"Gentlemen, good morning. In a moment, Alexandra Hughes, my assistant, is going to pass out a memo I've put together outlining the steps this department is going to take to mitigate the damage Revival's bass player, Indigo Hawk, known as Blue, has done to the network's reputation, as well as what we're going to do differently going forward to assure nothing like this ever happens again."

Bella paused. A long pause. I had to sit back in my seat in admiration. She really had nerves of steel. Almost anyone, even the most seasoned executive, probably would have withered under the scrutiny of the network brass. But she wasn't at all. She shook her head as if waving away a pesky fly.

"I've taken the liberty," she continued, "of putting together a short visual presentation that will put last night's performance in context."

Like we were in a theater, the room went nearly black. Then light flashed behind me. I had to swivel in my chair to take in the screen that emerged from behind wood-paneled doors. My assistant quickly ducked and took to the floor so her head wasn't blocking the screen. Isabella really had taken the seat of power.

I wasn't too close to appreciate the super-slick presentation that flashed across the screen.

Every bad word and every flash of skin was on display. It reminded me of my first year in America. That first year without Isabella to guide me. I thought I'd never get rid of my boner with the constant sex on display. There had been nothing like that in China. Culture shock hadn't really described it. It was as if my contraband manga had come to life.

The executives around the table didn't bat an eyelash. Instead there was nodding, some in self-satisfaction at the envelope-pushing scenes from CBT itself. Then, after all the more-or-less salacious content, was the flash of Blue's penis. It was amazing how that bit of skin looked like nothing when compared to the ten-minute skin fest we'd all just watched.

The lights went back on and there was a thick, stapled packet in front of me. I had to hand it to Bella, she was good. I'd been so busy watching the screen that I hadn't even noticed her assistant moving through the room.

"Gentlemen, going forward, we're going to be even more diligent when live shows come on the air. I propose increasing the time delay from seven seconds to fifteen. That should give anyone enough time to...edit what goes out across the airwaves."

Isabella's butt had barely hit the chair before the questions started. I had a few of my own, but decided to let those who'd been at the network far longer than me take the lead.

"What about the Family Viewing Council or Mother Knows Best?" one executive asked.

Bella's eyes narrowed barely a millimeter. Someone who didn't know her as well as I would scarcely have noticed it.

"What about them, Kevin? Ninety percent of the shows on our network were already on their shit list before Friday."

I scanned the faces of the men around the table, hoping to catch a glimpse of the irony here. We could swear. Almost everyone did in real life. Certainly half the viewing population had a penis, yet we were all dour-faced and seriously gathered around a conference room—on a freaking Saturday, of all days—talking about a glimpse of a penis like a giant F-bomb had landed in Utah.

"There's one reality show and one comedy they haven't come down on," Isabella continued. "During the upfronts, it was a point of pride that CBT was pushing the envelope. When you push it, sometimes it opens. I promise you, we'll seal it back up tighter than a nun's asshole."

"Will you respond to them?" asked another exec whose name I couldn't recall.

Isabella shook her head. She wasn't touching that one.

"Their formal letter to the network or the postcard campaign sure to rain down more than El Niño? I'll leave both to Legal."

I turned toward the lawyers, and their conservative-haircut heads bobbed in unison.

One of my father's associates stood next. He was one of the billionaires looking for a little glamour. Or rather, he'd found it. Liling had texted early this morning, picture of him in a comprising position around Drew O'Bryan's pool. I'd saved it to my phone like I know she'd done to hers. I'd make sure he was a yes vote on anything I put before the board.

"And the fines?" he asked. "We'll have to take a loss next quarter if the FCC is half as punitive as they've threatened to be after Howard Stern and Bubba the Love Sponge."

Before I knew it, I was standing and cashing in on that chit a little early.

I nodded towards my father's friend. "We think you've done an excellent job of putting last night's...incident...into context." It was a twofer. I hoped that Father's associate had gotten my hint. Then I looked at Bella, stared until her eyes met mine. For a second, before she masked it, there was a certain "deer in the headlights" look about her.

I watched her swallow the nonsense words that were surely churning in her brain. She went for the simple.

"Thank you," she started. "Alexandra Hughes did an excellent job overnight."

From Alexandra's own shocked face, I'd have bet a million of Father's easily earned dollars that it may have been her first compliment.

"So she did." I nodded. I stayed standing and let the quiet pause fill up the space. It was a game of "follow the leader." Kevin didn't pick up the baton.

"What about the fine?" he almost whined, as he could no doubt see his generous budget shrinking under the weight of the FCC. "Whose department is covering this?" He threw a wink at Isabella. "Of course *your* budget doesn't cover this."

I took note that Kevin Manning wasn't a team player, to file away later.

Isabella took the dig in stride. "Nope. Our money goes to salaries and pencils, Kevin. Past fines have been paid from Legal and Programming. I do hope that the FCC will minimize the fine, given that it was a live show and not scripted entertainment gone too far."

Then, like I was back in that schoolyard in Toms River, the adults in front of me started arguing. I watched, fascinated, for a good ten minutes before I put a stop to it.

"As a show of good faith, Woo DynoMedia will cover the fine. No one will have to sacrifice their budget," I said.

Though I was already thinking about whom CBT could well be rid of.

Isabella gasped at my offer. It was the first time I'd truly gotten her attention since I was here. I was thinking the millions were well worth it.

Budgets safe, the corporate execs fled like rats from a ship that might still sink under their slight weight.

Isabella's assistant probably wanted to flee, but held her ground, if hesitantly. "Isabella?"

"Wait for me in my office," Isabella barked at Alexandra.

At the order, the girl slumped. Even I could see that she was wrecked from probably having pulled an all-nighter. It couldn't have been easy gathering and editing all that footage.

"Go home," Isabella relented. "Get some sleep. I'll see you on Monday, okay? Thanks for all your help."

Bella's assistant didn't have to be told twice. She snatched up CDs and extra memos and exited as fast as her legs could take her. Again, Isabella and I were all alone. Only nine meters of highly polished wood separated us.

With no one but me around, Isabella deflated a little. When she let a bit of her guard down, I could see the girl I'd always loved.

"Isabella," I whispered. "Bella," came out on another breath.

"Don't call me that." She shook her head, defiantly trying to chase away the girl I'd met in New Jersey.

"Why not? It used to be my nickname for you." Isabella was her mother's daughter, a girl who Min Li alternately chastised or put down. Isabella was the woman before me wrapped in thousand-dollar designer armor.

"Jake, I have to go." She shrugged in minute apology for having a life outside of work. "Appointments and all that."

I couldn't let her go. I wasn't ready.

"I want to talk to you," I blurted, though I didn't have a thing to talk to her about. My mind was irritatingly blank.

As if obsequiousness were my due, Bella lowered her head a fraction. "Thanks for covering the fine. Really great of you and your dad."

Something about her posture pulled honesty from me. "I didn't do it for the network."

Abruptly, Isabella stood and pulled her portfolio to her chest like armor.

"Great. Well, I'm glad that you're starting your reign... um...tenure off on the right foot. You've bought yourself a lot of goodwill with that," she threw over her shoulder as she strode purposefully toward the door.

"What about you, Bella?" Her nickname halted her in her tracks. "Have I gotten into your good books?"

The moment the words were out, I knew they weren't the right ones. Too formal. Too...not me.

"My books are filled, Jake. We do best when we stay away from each other," she said. I wanted to protest, to say that it was the opposite—that we needed each other like two halves of a puzzle—to be whole. Her subsequent sigh was filled with resignation. "I'll get you an office. Then I think it would be best if we don't have anything to do with each other. My deputy, Connor Quinlan, has been in this department even longer than I have. I'm sure he can and will happily answer any questions you might have."

"I think there's one he can't answer." I took a step closer

to Bella. Then another. Then another. I knew she wouldn't run, even if she wanted to. The pretend daughter of Shorty Aconi never backed down from a challenge.

"What's that? I've got a couple of minutes."

She glanced at her watch in a way that told me she wasn't checking on the time of day. The timepiece was the twin of one Liling had. A rare Rolex that was easily half her salary. I got the hint, but didn't care. It was time to lay my cards on the table.

"Can we try again?"

From the look on Isabella's face, you'd have thought I'd pulled out a gun and aimed a shot at the ceiling rather than professing my true feelings.

"Have you lost your mind?" she shot back. "Did you eat blowfish or something over there in Asia that altered your brain chemistry?"

Her protective armor was still up. She wasn't hearing me. I tried plainer language.

"We once loved each other, Bella. I haven't met another woman who can replace you in my heart."

I wanted to backpedal, make some kind of preparations for what I was saying. But I hadn't known it was coming any more than she had.

"Have you green-lit a hidden-camera show? Am I your first victim—I mean guest? 'Cause then this might be funny." That latter she said with her New Jersey armor in full force.

I held up my hands in supplication. "I wouldn't joke about this, Bella."

"You and me...we were a disaster, remember?"

I remembered nothing of the kind. The circumstances *around* us had been a disaster. She and I had never been.

"You took my heart and trampled all over it."

Liling. Father. Min Li. I'd made so many mistakes that needed correcting.

"I'm not giving up. I expected you to act like this," I said, as if I'd had a plan all along. Needing to ease the sting of her rejection. "Knee-jerk reaction. I'll give you time to think about it. Let it settle in."

I left out the "me and you both" at the end there.

"Well *I* am. Giving up, that is," Isabella announced, then walked out of the room...her gold sandals stomping all over *my* heart this time.

CHAPTER 12

SIXTEEN YEARS EARLIER...

I CAN'T LIE. Those first months after Father sent me away were hard. Not too long after Bella and I had...discovered... our parents, I was shoehorned into the last free seat on a next plane to Shanghai. Father's driver picked me up at the airport and delivered me to the house I'd occupied the first thirteen years of my life.

Even though everything had been familiar, it hadn't really felt like home. Only our helper was there. She made me meals, but otherwise kept to herself.

I kept waiting for Min Li to show up, but she didn't. She may not have loved me, but at least it would have been someone to talk to. No such luck. It was nearly a month of excruciating boredom with me trying to figure out why *I* was being punished.

After a week of rereading all the manga I no longer had to hide, there wasn't much to do. Min Li hadn't exactly left a list of assignments.

Father wouldn't come to the phone, and my stomach

churned each time I called and Maria Aconi answered. I'd have tried Bella, but I didn't even know her phone number. The short walk between our houses had eliminated any need for electronic communication.

For a while, I practiced the piano and perfected the concerto I'd miss the recital for. Then I obsessively watched television coverage of the thousand-year bug, wondering if the lights would go out or planes would fall from the sky. None of it happened, which was too bad. The calamity would have been better than the nothing that filled my days.

When the helper announced I had a visitor, I nearly cried with relief. I hadn't really thought to fill a phone book with my friends' numbers before I left for New Jersey, and no one knew I was in town.

I didn't care if it was one of my father's old cronies, I'd gladly talk about business for as long as he'd stay.

But the person who walked through the door was too short and too young.

"Liling! What are you doing here?"

"Visiting."

I shooed out the helper with a request for some snacks and fruit juice.

"You have to tell everyone else I'm back. How is Ju Long? Quiang?"

Liling held up her hand. "Later. We can catch up on everyone later. We're going to have a lot of time."

"How long can you stay today? Maybe you can stay for dinner." I relished the prospect of not eating alone.

"I can only stay for a little while. I do have something for you, though."

"Manga?" I dropped my voice to a whisper. "Did you smuggle something in?"

I looked at her in her skirt and thin cardigan over a blouse. It didn't look like she could smuggle more than a piece of paper or two with those clothes.

Liling swung a small leather bag I hadn't seen from her back to her front, then took a seat on the edge of the living room chair.

"Here." She thrust a stack of what looked like mail toward me. "This is for you."

I took the slick envelope in one hand and small bound book in the other. I opened the envelope first. It was a plane ticket from Shanghai to New York City. My breath came out in a whoosh of relief.

I was going back.

I could be with Bella again, now that I'd finished my punishment or banishment or exile or whatever this had been.

"I never thought I'd say this, but I cannot wait to get back to New Jersey."

"I'll be flying with you. We'll have fifteen hours together."

"If you bring something to read..." I didn't care how long the plane ride was. All I cared about was the destination.

"You should look at this." She picked up the little booklet and put it in my hand.

It was in English. An American or British school brochure, from the looks of the kids of every color lying across a big green lawn, surrounded by multicolored trees in autumn and a bunch of older brick buildings.

Woodward Tillman spilled across the cover in big type.

"What is this?"

"It's where I go to school."

I closed my eyes for a second, trying to remember something Father had said. "I forgot. You're in school in America. Cool. Maybe I'll see you sometime," I said.

That last had been just to be polite. My mind and the rest of my body was yearning to get back to Toms River. I was already working out how Bella and I could be more careful. I'd make sure that none of our parents caught us next time. Because surely all I could think about as I held these tickets in my hand was that there was definitely going to be a next time when we could be alone together.

"You're coming with me."

"Now?" I pulled the tickets closer to my nose and squinted. The flight was five days away.

As if Liling could hear my thoughts, she nodded her head.

"Next week. You'll be coming with me...to Woodward Tillman."

"What?"

"You're going to start there in a few weeks. We're going to be at school together again! It'll be like old times!" Liling's thin arms flapped in excitement.

I didn't want old times. I wanted my life in New Jersey back. I'd happily put up with Evan and Cole and Min Li and piano and Mandarin just to be a few meters from Bella again.

"Together?" I asked. I was trying to wrap my head around the abrupt shift from what I thought would be to what was going to be, undoubtedly a command direct from Father. Liling was an unwitting messenger. A character in a play she hadn't auditioned for. He knew I wouldn't put up a protest. Not in front of the daughter of one of his business associates. I'd been indoctrinated enough to know that keeping up appearances was always paramount.

"You aren't the only person living in America. About half the kids from our old school are enrolled there. Everybody wants their kids to learn English."

"You too?"

"Me too. My father wants me to learn how Americans do things and come back to help him with Red Dragon."

Liling's dad was dead set on getting government approval to run a television network. He was as convinced that media was the future as Father was that selling Chinese-made consumer goods in American would make many Chinese billionaires.

"So what's it like?" I asked while blowing out a breath. Dad was sending me away to keep me from Bella, or to keep me from telling Min Li about Maria, or both. But I could figure out a way to see Bella. A couple hundred kilometers wasn't an ocean.

"It's okay. Kind of fun actually. The work isn't too hard."

"What's the fun part?"

"No parents."

"What do you mean?"

"It's boarding school. There are like six hundred students and like fifty adults. They mostly go home at night and we can do what we want."

"Read manga?"

"All I can get up from New York."

"You go to New York City?"

"There are free weekends. I take the train down."

This was going to be even easier than I thought. I'd go to this place with its perfect-looking teenagers and unblemished lawns, then I'd figure out how to meet Bella on my first free weekend.

"Maybe you can help me pack."

"Let's see what's in your stash."

I led the way. She could take all the manga she wanted. I was going back home.

CHAPTER 13

SIXTEEN YEARS EARLIER...

CLOTHES WERE in a trunk in my triple room and a shiny new MacBook was on my desk when I got out of the limo at the school. The head of the school welcomed me himself. I was a week early for the start of the new semester, and Liling was staying with some family friends. I ate dinner with his family while he gave me a personal orientation and I got over my jet lag.

The moment I opened the laptop and plugged it into the school's network, I got on the internet and checked my Mind-Spring e-mail. Bella and I had signed up for accounts one day in Father's office.

"If we're ever separated," she'd said.

"For secret messages," I'd said.

We'd both been eerily prescient. The minute I signed in, a list of at least fifty messages had filled the screen. They'd gone from mild questioning to increasingly frantic, to calm when her mother had relayed that I was to be in exile at boarding school.

I'd look at the other messages later. I'd opened the last one first.

ICQ me, it had said. That missive had been followed by a long string of numbers.

Took me about an hour to figure out what ICQ was, how to download it to the computer, to wait for the download, then install it. I got my own ID, which was an even longer string of numbers. After a last dinner with the headmaster, and a younger guy who was going to be my World Literature teacher as well as my housemaster, I rushed back to the room and messaged Isabella.

That first night, we were online for hours. She'd nearly gotten into trouble when Father had spotted the late-night glow from the guesthouse. After that, we'd agreed to only message when Father was either sleeping or on the phone and Maria Aconi was safely glued to *Oprah*.

The next night I was nervously pacing in my dorm room. I'd already read and reread all of Bella's ICQ messages and finally all of her emails besides. There was a lot of time to fill until school started in a few days. I was surprised when a knock came close to nine o'clock. Too late for the head of school or dean of students or any of the other students who were tasked with welcoming me. I opened the door to see who it could be.

"Nervous?" It was Liling at the door. She was in school sweats, a t-shirt, and a zip-up sweater that hung open. The thin white shirt she was wearing clung to breasts I'd never noticed. She wasn't wearing a bra.

My dick stirred uncomfortably in my pants. I'd known she was a girl. She'd been a girl since the first moment I'd met her in school when we were both little. But the difference between us was more apparent than it had ever been.

Suddenly I *was* nervous, and it had nothing to do with Woodward Tillman.

"My roommates still aren't here."

"A bunch of kids don't come over the weekend if they don't have Monday classes."

"You can come in, I guess."

"They've got you in a triple. Cool. It's good to always have someone to go to dinner with."

"Gotta be better than the headmaster."

"Oh, God. I should have come back earlier to keep you company. Was it boring?"

"Not too bad. Once his family realized I could speak English, it wasn't so awkward. That first night, everyone spoke so slowly, I thought something was wrong with them."

Liling's laugh was loud and hearty. She pulled the black elastic from her hair and shook it around her shoulders, covering her long, slim neck. Unexpectedly, I wanted to kiss that neck.

She kicked off her shoes. Her feet were bare.

"Let me guess which is yours." She pointed toward the only bed that would have blended in with the wallpaper at Father's Toms River house. "Shiny blue with that hideous pattern on it."

"You win."

She sat down on the twin and pulled the window firmly closed. I was instantly warmer, though I couldn't totally credit the lack of fresh, cold January air.

"It's kind of Chinese. You should go into town and get

something boring and blue." She pointed to the other beds. "Like these guys."

"Town?"

"There's a bus every day. You can get stuff from the Marshalls at the end of the line. There's a drugstore and snacks and stuff closer in."

"I'll go next weekend."

"I can come with you, if you want. I think my taste may be more...American...than your mom's."

"It's okay to say it. Min Li leans toward the tacky. You should see the house in New Jersey. It's an assault on the eyes."

"Since when do you call your mom by her name?"

Since I found out my mom wasn't my mom, I wanted to say. That kind of admission would ruin the careful family image that was so important to Father. If I were honest, it's the kind of secret that, if revealed, would only make my life more difficult. Bella and I didn't need anything to be more difficult.

"Since they sent me to Shanghai."

"What *did* you do? Father wouldn't tell me."

I sat down next to her, leaning my back against the window. There was no answer I could give. I didn't want to talk about Bella. I couldn't talk about my father or Maria Aconi.

"I was getting behind in my music, Mandarin. They were worried about what kind of influence the public school was having," I lied.

Liling shook the sweater from her shoulders, then ran a hand up and down my arm. I felt her touch against every nerve ending, even through the thick cotton of my own long-sleeved tee. Wind rattled the window behind me. A draft escaped. I couldn't help but notice that her nipples, brown against the stark white shirt, were pulled hard and tight underneath.

Shit. I needed to do something. To say something that would break the spell that nighttime and loneliness and familiarity were weaving around us.

I popped up from the bed and started rummaging around the room.

"You want a drink?" I asked. "I think I saw a bottle of some kind of liqueur on the shelf."

Liling nodded, but didn't say anything further. I found a couple of small paper cups, twisted open the bottle and poured each of us a drink. I sipped and tried not to frown at the taste. It was like licorice candy in a cup. Following Liling's lead, I drank the rest in a single swallow. I poured each of us a second serving, before I closed the bottle and replaced it on one of my soon-to-be roommates' shelves. We each drank. I crumpled my cup and heaved it toward a wastebasket.

"And he scored," I whisper-shouted in my fake sports announcer voice.

"And she missed," Liling said as her crumpled cup fell short of its target.

Even though I'd eaten dinner, the alcohol went to my head pretty quickly. I didn't feel quite dizzy, but my head wasn't the same as it had always been. I'd had a couple of sips of Baijiu from Father's cabinet during parties, but never this much at one time. I looked at Liling. Her eyes were a bit glassy. We'd had the same amount, but she probably weighed a good twenty kilos lighter than me.

"There's something I need to tell you," Liling whispered. She leaned over toward me so we were touching from head to shoulder.

"What?"

"I've always had a crush on you. Since we were little. You never really noticed me. I..."

Then Liling did the most unexpected thing. She scooted so that her legs straddled my hips, then she put her lips against mine. That first touch was as soft as a butterfly and nearly as tentative.

I wanted to pull away. But I couldn't summon Bella like I had every night since I'd left New Jersey. I'd missed her so much. The sting of waking up every day thousands of miles away had been like a knock to my heart every day. Getting to Bella seemed like less of a reality with every sunrise and sunset without her.

I looked at Liling who was here. Now. There was no Father or Min Li doing everything in their power to keep us apart. I'd been naïve when I'd landed in Newark. Somehow I thought I'd get on a bus or a train and go straight home. But that had been forbidden.

Here and now, I couldn't think of anything but the warm and willing girl in front of me who tasted like spice. I shifted forward and wrapped my arms around her neck. I slanted and made it into a real kiss. Her lips were softer than I'd imagined, not that I had really thought much about them. Her tongue made me harder than I ever remembered being. She tasted like vanilla and the Jägermeister. Distractedly, I wondered what in the heck made her taste like American desserts.

"I want you to be my first, Wu Jian."

"You've never..."

"Have you?"

I shook my head. Suddenly, I very much wanted to be her first.

"Do you have a girlfriend?" she asked.

Very slowly, I shook my head again, wiping Bella away with each movement of my head. When her name would have escaped my lips, I pressed them to Liling's. What I wanted in New Jersey and what was real right here in front of me were two completely different things.

"Thank goodness. I was so worried that you'd find someone here in America."

I didn't want to talk about any of that, so I pulled her heavy, dark hair behind her back and kissed her again. I let go of her hair and fit my hands around her waist, under her shirt.

She pulled back and lifted the shirt over her head. I'd been right that she hadn't worn a bra. Liling lifted my hands in hers and placed them on her breasts. Her nipples beaded hard against my palms. I couldn't help but squeeze each hand. My God, it was amazing, the feeling that arrowed straight to my dick.

Pushing her down on the silky cover, I licked my way toward one nipple and pulled it deep into my mouth. So good. My brain nearly short-circuited. When she moaned, I swear I lost all thought.

I sucked again, and she moaned louder. I didn't think it

possible, but I was getting harder by the minute. My balls were near full to bursting.

With a pop, I took my mouth from her and repeated the lick and suck on the other side. I sat up and pulled off my own shirt. The sound of shifting against the covers was her removing her sweats. I stood and made sure the lock on the door was tight, then shucked my own jeans and sneakers. Liling welcomed me back with her legs wide and arms open.

Before I knew what I was doing, I'd fisted myself and was rubbing my cock up and down the warm, wet space between her legs.

One moment I was thinking about how good it would feel to sink inside her, and in the next, I was doing just that.

"Oooh...oh!" she gasped.

"Is this okay?" I asked. Not that I'd have been able to do anything other than sink deeper inside her if she'd asked.

I felt and saw her nod. As if I were being controlled by some kind of puppet strings, I pulled out and slipped in again. It was so tight. She was so much tighter than I'd expected a girl to be. The feeling was incredible, indescribable. Suddenly, wars made a lot of sense.

"You're so..." I reached for a word. "Creamy." It was the only one that came to mind.

"I...I've always wanted only you, Jian," she said, every word came out on a pant.

"I can't... Oh God." Two or three more pumps and my balls squeezed tight, shooting my load much faster than I would have wanted.

Immediately, I pulled out and rolled away toward the cold window.

Faster than I could have said Liling's name, guilt descended over me.

Bella.

I'd wanted us to be each other's firsts.

"I'm sorry," I said to the ceiling. I threw an arm over my eyes. The overhead light seemed suddenly harsh against my irises.

"I'm not. It will be better next time."

"Next time?"

"That's what my roommate says."

"You asked your roommate about sex?"

"American girls know a lot about this sort of thing. She gave me the guts to come over here tonight."

The doorknob jostled.

"Who...? Jesus!"

Liling slipped her shirt and pants on as fast as she could, but it wasn't fast enough. Her underpants slowed her down. Her legs were spread, nothing hidden, when the door gave way and two boys nearly tumbled in. I snatched my own underwear and pants and pulled up both at the same time. I was tucked, zipped, and buttoned in a matter of seconds.

"We never lock—"

"Holy shit! The Panda's getting laid!"

It was Cole. Cole Lehman. I fully expected Evan to be pulling up the rear, but I didn't recognize the boy behind him at all. "Abbott. Meet Jian...something. Jake Wu. He's followed me here all the way from Jersey."

I looked toward Liling. Thank God she'd managed the elastic of her underwear. She was pulling the cord of her sweats tight and zipping her hooded sweater to her neck.

"I've gotta go before lights out," she said before jamming her feet into her laced shoes and shuffling from the room.

"Nice snatch," Abbott said. "I'd do her. So you guys already know each other?" He dropped a duffle on a striped white and navy comforter. That was his bed, I guess.

Cole closed the door and kicked his own leather weekend backpack toward it. "Jake Wu. Man, I didn't expect to see you. I got some kind of letter saying we had a new roommate, but I forgot to read that shit. What in the hell are you doing here?"

"My dad thinks that public school isn't good enough anymore."

"I feel you, man. Where's your watchdog?"

Abbott stopped pulling crap from his bag and watched the back and forth between us like it was a show.

"Bella's still in Jersey." My stomach contracted at the mention of her name.

To Abbott, Cole said, "He's got this girl, man. She's no joke. All Mafia connected and shit. Lives next door to him or something."

Cole's buddy act was disconcerting. While I felt kind of naked around him without Bella, he wasn't nearly as much of an ass without Evan behind him.

He took my hand in his and did a bro handshake. I was only able to keep up because I'd seen it on American TV. It was his way, I think, of calling a truce. Silently, I accepted.

"So who's this Bella?" Abbott asked.

"Cute girl, in a Jersey kind of way. You hitting that, too?"

Scared to lose the tiny bit of street cred I'd built when they'd walked in on a naked Liling, I nodded slightly.

"Man, I'm not sure what this Panda shit was that Cole was slinging. But you're one to milk a situation. Pussy back home *and* here. Fucking-A, man. Lily wasn't giving it up to *anyone*. You're here not five minutes and she's under you. Looked hot as shit, man. Going to have to add that image of her to my spank bank."

Pulling my basket of shampoo and soap from the windowsill, I stood. "I gotta shower."

"Yeah, we'll open the windows. Get the smell of sex out of here. Otherwise I'm gonna have to sleep with my dick in my hand," Cole said, waving his hand in front of his nose.

Suddenly in a hurry, I snatched a towel from my cubby and made my way to the bathroom. Guilt and something else ate at me, hard. I needed some hot-ass water to scrub those feelings away.

CHAPTER 14

SIXTEEN YEARS EARLIER...

"YOUR COMPUTER IS LIGHTING up like a Christmas tree," Abbott Gordon said to me while passing in the hall. He was one of my two roommates at Woodward Tillman. The third was none other than Cole...Coleton Lehman. Somehow the administration thought moving me in with someone from Toms River would make my introduction to this school better.

Without Isabella there to fight my battles, Cole and I had come to a sort of truce. Father had said that keeping the right kind of people on my good side would benefit the family and our businesses down the road.

Though his immediate family wasn't in finance, Father said that they were living off profits from the New York firm while using their family's private equity fund to invest in various companies. I took him at his word and did my best to forget New Jersey Cole and embrace Woodward Tillman Cole.

My progress to our triple slowed considerably after

Abbott's comment. I knew who the messages would be from. There was only one person who messaged me through my laptop, a near duplicate of hers—Isabella Aconi. Every other day or so, I was deliberately out of my room at four thirty. I told Bella that it was school keeping me busy. That was only half true.

Liling was the other half of that truth.

I didn't love Liling. I knew that. I also knew that I was probably using her. But I couldn't quit her. She gave herself to me without strings. For now, I was taking what was offered. I pushed aside the double whammy of guilt for not being what either girl needed.

I woke the laptop.

"I got it!" Isabella had typed.

I unpacked my backpack. Changed from the uniform of khakis and button-down shirt into school-issued navy sweats and a t-shirt. Had a glass of water. Then sat down at my desk. I had to wake the laptop again.

"Your license???" I couldn't think of a single other thing my father hadn't already bought her. My father and her mother were using a lot of expensive gifts to buy her silence.

I wanted to tell them that it wasn't the least bit necessary. No way would either of us have blabbed. It would have surely meant Maria Aconi would be fired and banished from New Jersey, along with Bella as collateral damage. Not one of the four of us wanted that.

Bella: Yes!!!!!!!!!!!!!!

Jake: I still can't believe he gave you a car.

Bella: I know, right?

Abbott came back in with a bag of something in orange polypropylene. He ripped it open and spilled the snack out on paper towels on his own desk. The smell alternated between gross and enticing.

"What in the hell is that?" I asked. I stood and poked a pencil at the nuclear red-orange shapes on Abbott's desk.

"Flamin' Hot Cheetos, man. They are like the best thing ever. I had them when I was interning in Philly last summer for that nonprofit. I finally got the school to stock them in the vending machines."

"Is that the thing you were writing all the letters about?"

I never knew where Abbott was coming from. Half the time he was writing letters to the editor of the *New York Times*, protesting one thing or another. The rest of the time he was writing letters for personal gain. To get free stuff from J. Crew, return year-old electronics to Costco, or get the school do something they didn't want to.

Abbott nodded, his brown hair flopping over his blue-gray eyes. "When I first asked, they said it wasn't a good idea to add another non-nutritional snack. They were going to add like apples or something instead. Like there wasn't already enough fruit in this place."

"Fruit is good." Although fruit in a vending machine did sound like a bad idea on a campus full of teens.

"You'd say that. I've never seen anyone eat that much melon until you moved in."

I'd never seen this much year-round melon until I'd moved to America. It had been my favorite summer treat as a kid, and even though it wasn't very good or sweet, I couldn't pass it up in my search for that perfect taste from my boyhood. I didn't say any of that. I'd learned, ironically from Cole, that no one wanted to hear about China.

"So what happened?"

Abbott did blink in surprise at my interest. Normally I put on headphones and tuned out his long, rambling tales of vindication of the political or retail kind. He continued with amped-up enthusiasm.

"I did some research. Did you know that these were invented by a janitor at Frito-Lay? He's like a total Horatio Alger story. He's one of eleven kids. Picked grapes. Dropped out of high school. Became a janitor. Invented these."

Abbott held up one of the oblong snacks.

"Now he's like a VP of the Hispanic market or something. I wrote all that up, presented it to the dean of students and voila, they added them because it contributes to the school's diversity, equity, and social justice initiative. And I get to enjoy a really good snack."

He crammed about five of the pieces in his mouth and unscrewed an orange soda. I tried not to think about what that combination would do to the lining of his stomach.

Abbott swallowed. "Want one? They're the best ever."

"Dinner is soon. I need to get back..." Guilt gnawed at me.

"To your Jersey girl? You tell her you have a Woodward girl?"

"I don't have a Woodward girl."

"Whoa, ho. Maybe you should tell that to Lily. I'm sure she's on her way to the dining hall to hold down a table for you. Probably got white linen and candles all ready."

I wished Abbott was exaggerating. Liling had made it her

job to make my life easier at Woodward. In addition to regular sex, she made sure my favorite foods were put aside in the cafeteria, that my favorite study carrel was available in the library, that my laundry was always clean and folded. It was what I imagined it was like having a wife, one that never complained or had demands of her own.

I wasn't sure what she got out of the relationship, but whenever I asked, she just smiled, nodded, and asked me what I needed. Since we were only sixteen, it was a relief that marriage, at least, was off the table. I mostly took her at her word that making me happy made *her* happy.

"Lily...she's a family friend," I hedged. "Our fathers knew each other in Shanghai."

I left out the part where we'd once been best friends with secrets, kind of like Bella and me, before the power in our relationship had shifted to where it was now, slightly off-kilter.

"Do you fuck all your family friends? 'Cause I gotta get more friendly with my dad's friends' daughters, then."

"Eat your orange food." I turned back to the computer. At this point, Bella seemed easier than Abbott or Liling.

Jake: Has he asked anything about us?

Bella: He has to know I got the laptop to e-mail you. Then again, maybe not. Your dad's not a detail guy.

Jake: Did he restrict where you can drive?

How did you break up with someone you'd never really gone out with? In person? Did I have to break up with Bella if we'd never been together? It wasn't like Lily and I had ever had that "define the relationship" conversation either. She'd come in that Sunday a few months back and repeated it nearly every Sunday since, then everyone around us had started treating us kind of like a couple.

Not privy to my thoughts, the little cursor followed Bella's words across the screen.

Bella: Nope. He gave me a credit card, though. For gas and other stuff. I've taken the girls to dinner at Bennigan's a couple of times. He hasn't said anything.

Jake: Dad's never said anything about my credit card either. As long as I bring home straight A's, I can do whatever I want.

Bella: Glad you like it there.

Jake: It would totally freak out your mom and my dad if you drove up here, wouldn't it?

Bella: LOL. It totally would. But what could they say?

Jake: Probably nothing. We hold all the cards.

Bella: Totally American slang.

Jake: You're not my only source.

Bella: You know what? I'm coming.

Jake: Now isn't a good time for visitors. Spring break is only four days at Easter.

I shut the computer, as quickly as I could before she could press the issue. Having shut down the conversation about a visit, I was relieved I'd put off a face-to-face conversation with Isabella for at least a week, if not more. With that last line, I'd left room to not visit home and see her over the short Easter break. Graduation would be a couple of weeks after that. By then, I'd have figured out Liling or Isabella or both.

"Ready for dinner?" I asked Abbott.

"Yeah. I'm good. Need to get something else in me."

"You think?"

"The kids in that New Hope program would eat this for lunch. No meat or salad or anything. I'm not sure how they keep going just on junk."

My mind flashed to the children begging near the Bund. "Some kind of government programs?"

"Yeah, probably. Do you know what's on the menu for tonight?"

"Probably burgers or something." I hated the weekend menus. I was getting pretty tired of American food in general. None of it was as good as Shanghai food, or even Maria Aconi's.

I was relieved that Lily wasn't in the dining hall. I checked my phone. Sure enough, there was a text from her apologizing for not coming to dinner. She was working on a big final project with a group. I tried not to sigh in relief.

"Not hungry?" Cole asked. He and a few of his lacrosse teammates had joined me and Abbott at our table in the dining hall.

"The scent of those cheese things threw me off."

Like I'd hoped, Abbott launched into a long story about how he'd pulled one over on the Dean and no one noticed what I was or wasn't eating. Sometimes these guys were like mother hens. That ate like wolves though, and soon enough we were walking back across campus up to the dorms. When I checked the computer there wasn't anything else from Isabella.

Relieved, I showered, got into bed, and picked up *The*

Age of Innocence. I had a paper due in a week and I'd yet to make it past the first chapter. Saturday was a rinse and repeat of the day before, without classes.

After dinner, we all made our way upstairs. The guys were busy boasting about how and who they were going to hook up with over the weekend. I knew it was all talk. Most likely they'd all end up working on their end-of-term projects because ninety-nine percent of the girls at the school were doing the same.

"There's a present in your bed," Abbott shouted from our room. He'd been the first in the door, with Cole and me bringing up the rear. Two of the guys from dinner were in the hall as well, having not gotten to their door yet.

I craned my neck, trying to figure out what Liling was playing at. There was a loud thud as my hardcover copy of the Edith Wharton book hit the floor. All of us fell into the room like a heap of puppies. Too much testosterone for the hundred-year-old doorframe.

To say I was shocked to see Bella was an understatement. I had to shift my expectation from one girl to another. Before I could get one word out, Isabella was bellowing a greeting.

"Coleton Lehman, you asshole. What are you doing here?"

The back of my neck was feeling warm. The heat in these old buildings was always turned to maximum. I'd heard they had a coal-fired boiler somewhere down the hill. I pulled at the collar of my shirt, trying to let in some air as my gaze shifted to the guys around me. How had her accent gotten so strong in the last few months? She sounded like a caricature of someone on *The Sopranos.*

A little smile played around Cole's mouth, and I knew he heard the same thing I did. Cole had been in New Jersey for more years than Bella, but he sounded like a CNN news anchor.

"Playing lacrosse," he answered.

"Fucking-A," Bella shot back, her ponytail barely moved even though she was gesticulating like mad. "I assume you're not shitting on Jake. I wouldn't want to have to come up here and whup ass."

The room filled with the laughter of boys whose voices had recently changed to sound like the men they'd soon become.

"Whup ass?" one of his teammates said in a dead near imitation of either Isabella or Carmela Soprano.

Oblivious, Isabella thumped her chest like she was going to have a street fight in any moment. "I can bring it. I wouldn't laugh so fast if I were you."

Before this turned into some kind of impromptu theater, I needed to get out of here with Isabella.

"You hungry?" I asked her, making my way to the bed, hoping to block her in all her fully made-up and hot-pink-sweat suited glory from their view.

She stood. I could see some kind of rhinestones glittering on her butt. Neither Lily nor any of the girls around here would be caught dead looking like this anytime outside of a formal dance, and maybe not even then.

"Starving." She rubbed at her stomach like she hadn't eaten in days and not hours. "I haven't eaten since breakfast."

My neck was burning again. It was way too quiet in the room as the guys took in the spectacle that was Isabella. I started toward the door, throwing the words over my shoulder.

"Let's go get something to eat, then."

Bella tossed her new keys into the air. The collection of key chains hanging on the fob clinked like a girl's charm bracelet. Only this one had a Mercedes *and* a BMW medallion. I knew she was driving a car from Father's company, shipped new from China. It wasn't either of those German cars. I decided not to ask about that, or the unnaturally purple rabbit's foot.

I clattered down the narrow, creaky old wood steps. Rumor has it that our room was probably a maid's room once. I took the second set two by two. Cooler outside air would help me feel a lot better, I hoped. Once out the front door, we stood awkwardly for a moment.

She pointed toward one of the faculty lots, and I followed her to the red SUV. The car blooped once when Isabella pointed her big mess of metal and keys toward the door. Then it chimed again when the doors unlocked and the interior lights came on. No doubt this show went over big with her New Jersey friends.

I pulled open the passenger door and got in the car. The smell of the air freshener dangling from the rearview mirror was overpowering.

"What's good around here?" she asked while backing out of the space. She was careful to make sure that she cleared the real Mercedes and BMWs students had left in the lot for the weekend.

"Italian," I said without thinking. It's what Liling and I had when we went out.

"Seriously? What else?" she asked. "Please don't say Chinese."

I knew she thought that was a joke. For some reason, I was having a hard time finding Isabella amusing. I fished through my head for the few restaurants in town. Some of the guys liked to go out on the weekends. I didn't think the restaurant food was considerably better than the dorm food, but went along about half the time. I think the real reason they liked to go out was because none of the bartenders or wait staff looked too closely at fake IDs, if they carded at all.

"There's a burger place that's really good." I had no idea if the burgers were good. All I knew was that they'd serve minors and, right now, I really wanted a beer. I needed something to make me feel better.

Isabella considered for a moment. I expected a protest, but got none.

"Point and I'll drive," she said.

I did, and ten minutes later, we'd parked and entered the establishment. What it lacked in atmosphere it made up for with darkness. We took one of the empty wood tables in the back away from the other clumps of students. Some I recognized. The rest were probably from the other two boarding schools in the neighboring towns.

I took the menu proffered and looked through the offerings, picking the one thing I thought would soak up the beer best.

None of the things I wanted to say were a good idea. I decided to start with the truth.

"I didn't really think you'd come." I dropped my menu and signaled to the waitress with my raised hand.

"Why not?" The bellicose Isabella from my dorm room was replaced with an earlier version of herself, quiet, tentative. "I wanted to see you and I have a car. And a license. It was a total no-brainer."

She fiddled with the menus. I resisted the urge to put my hand on top of hers, stopping the nervous movement. Even that slight touch, I knew, might give her the wrong idea.

"How long are you planning to stay?" If she got on the road in a couple of hours, then everything could go back to normal. I'd finish *Age of Innocence*, or at least finish the paper. Liling would probably be none the wiser. It would kind of be like this visit had never happened.

For a long moment, Isabella sat back in her chair.

"What's up? You sound like you're behind a motel desk." Then she straightened. Cleared her throat. Blinked her darkly lined eyes slowly. "I'm planning on checking in this afternoon." Her voice was deep, mock authoritative. "I'll check out tomorrow. What's your checkout time?" I could see a hint of a smile she could barely hide. I'd seen the expression so many times before. It had made my stomach fill with butterflies or my dick twitch in my pants. Right now, I didn't feel much of anything. I'd wanted this so bad for so long that guilt crushed me. I couldn't figure out what had changed, but something was profoundly different between us. I'd planned on going to her. Being with her. Then going to her and explaining why we couldn't be. Now, the feeling in my stomach wasn't butterflies, but a pit filled with something that felt like the end of a long-held dream.

Had we always been so different. I didn't want Min Li to have been right.

"What did you tell your mother?" I asked, because Maria Aconi was the equivalent of a cold bucket of water.

"Since when do you give a shit what Maria Sofia thinks? I told her I was staying at a friend's. All of that is one hundred percent true."

I didn't tell Isabella that her annoyed face was practically a carbon copy of her mother's.

"What about when my dad gets a gas charge for New York or Connecticut?"

"You said yourself, he doesn't check. I'm not going to worry about fifty or sixty dollars in gas. I wanted to see you."

I tried not to let the whining note in her voice grate on me. Liling was practically an expert at a soft voice and considered delivery. No matter what I did, she was never annoyed with me.

"We haven't been able to have a minute alone since forever."

I was relieved when the waitress came over. I ordered pork wings and a beer.

Isabella got a cheeseburger.

"That's it? You aren't going to try the pulled pork or something?"

It was like she didn't even want to try stretching her wings. Liling would have ordered the most exotic thing on the menu, then cheerily commented on odd American sensibilities.

"I know what a burger's like. I'll stick with that." She pulled my hands in hers. That feeling for her, the one I'd thought was dead or was only guilt, morphed a little bit with this contact. She pulled me close. Her strawberry gloss and Tic Tac breath was so familiar.

"I can't believe you ordered a beer."

I pulled my hands back, wiped my suddenly sweaty palms on my khakis. I hoped breaking contact would break the spell that made me feel like she had a hold on me.

"It's near a school. They never card."

The first beer came before dinner and went down easy. I didn't particularly like the taste, but I wanted to dull the feelings swirling around me and this was as good as any underage kid was going to get. I told her about Abbott's vending machine victory, and Cole's lacrosse games. I didn't really care about either but wanted to steer clear of anything that could touch on us. I knew what Isabella wanted. I knew what she'd come here for. She'd left hints like breadcrumbs through our chats.

She'd turned down every guy who'd asked her out. She'd been saving her virginity for me. She wanted us to lose ours to each other. I certainly wasn't going to tell her that I'd already done that dance with Liling. That, now that I was at Woodward, I could see what Min Li and my father said was true.

Not all of it. Not the stuff about Isabella never amounting to more than a housekeeper. But the other parts. That we were from different worlds entirely. That any relationship we had would hit a dead end. Though it was clear from watching her with my friends that we'd already crashed into that dead end, neither of us was willing to acknowledge it.

When I was done with my third beer, and Isabella was done picking through her dinner, I motioned for the check.

Paying was the least I could do to keep from rousing suspicion.

"What do you have to do to get your roommates out of your room for the night?"

I took a deep breath and let it out. This was the exact thing I was worried about. I should have spent more time thinking about how I was going to rebuff her invitation and less time drinking. I certainly hadn't found the answer in three beers.

Isabella had relaxed some. I could see more of the old her under the makeup and rhinestone-studded clothes. I could see a path easier than honesty, and I chose it. I fished my phone from my pocket and hit Cole's number. If Abbott was behaving in character, he'd have turned off his phone to study hours ago.

"Lehman."

"Can you guys clear out?"

"Oooh. Someone's going to get laid. The Wimpy Panda is showing his bear claws. Or big bear dick, maybe. I wonder how big panda dicks are."

"Just do it," I said then hung up before Cole got Abbott involved and they went down a research rabbit hole of comparative Ursidae penis size.

I didn't say anything to Isabella on the way back to campus except to point when she needed to turn. I tried not to smile when it took her five minutes to pull between the lines of the only available parking space. There, for a moment, was a glimpse of what I used to love about her. Three chocolate stouts had not been the best idea. Drunk dick was a thing I'd heard of, but never experienced. Maybe I could convince her that we should sleep together and not *sleep* together.

When she finally turned off the car with a triumphant smile, I pulled at the handle and jumped from the open door. Mentally, I perused the not-so-secret collection of magazines stored in Cole's closet. I could do this. For so long, I'd wanted to do this more than anything in the world, and now everything about us seemed like the run up Peak Drive to Castle Craig that we'd had to do in P.E.

Gravel crunched under our feet, then the sound of one set of feet got quieter.

Sometime in the last couple of minutes, Isabella had reversed direction. She had all her keys and chains rattling in her hand before the car again made a noise as the alarm disengaged and the doors unlocked. She hoisted herself into the SUV with the handle and slammed the door. There was no spray of rocks because the car didn't move. I could hear muffled sounds of her favorite grunge band, but nothing more. I watched as the dome light came on and her face turned toward the gear shift.

She was leaving.

It was all my fault. I'd been a complete ass from the moment I'd seen her sleeping in my bed. I should have had a conversation with her. Broken up the thing we'd never had. Maybe changed the nature of our relationship so we could keep on being friends.

I'd wanted my father to treat me like a man. Now it was time to start acting like one. I strode toward the cherry-red car and banged on the driver-side window. After a bit of fumbling, Isabella found the right button. The window eased down with a soft mechanical whir.

"What, Jake?"

"Where are you going?"

"Home." Her face was a mask of uncertainty and sadness. I'd put that there. It was my job to erase it. "I obviously crashed whatever you've got going on here. I figured I would do you the favor and head home."

"You can't leave in the night. Drive in the dark." I'd done a few unforgiveable things in the last months, but if this girl, a clearly inexperienced driver, died on the highway between here and New Jersey, Maria Aconi would come up here and kill me herself.

"Why not? The expressways are open. Certainly the toll booths are twenty-four hours. Why shouldn't I turn around and go back from where I came? I'll take with me the lesson not to surprise people. Only come when you're invited."

"Turn off the car," I said. I'd made a decision.

I pulled the handle and she fell out into my arms. Warm, sweet Bella. My first love was in my arms, sad, unmoored, uncertain. I needed to fix this. I needed to make this better. I needed to love her like she deserved.

"Bella."

CHAPTER 15

SIXTEEN YEARS EARLIER...

THIS TIME...THIS time I did everything right. I took the fob from her hand. I pulled her close when she shivered. I pressed the button that unlatched the trunk. Letting her go, I pulled out her wheelie bag and duffle she'd packed. So many clothes for one night. She must have been more nervous than I'd thought.

I opened the door of Baxter Hall, noticing for only the second time how unobtrusive the signs were here. It was as if New England were reluctant to announce itself to the world. How out of place Bella must have felt, trying to find her way around the warren of buildings and hedges and ivy.

At least Cole and Abbott had made good on their promise. The room was empty when we got there. I turned off the harsh overhead light and pulled the chain on the floor lamp next to my bed. I flicked through Abbott's CD collection and put Creed in his boom box. The first haunting notes of "With Arms Wide Open" filled the room. That boom box was our agreed-upon sign that we were not to be disturbed for any reason. Cole had used it. I had used it with Liling. I don't think Abbott had, though he's the one who'd devised the system.

I pulled her to me as tightly as I could.

"I'm sorry." I buried my nose in her hair. "So sorry, Bella." I *was* sorry. For my father. For her mother. For Liling. For my asshole friends here at Woodward who could smell a class difference a mile away.

For the sake of her pride, I pretended to ignore the tears.

"You can't let my dad or your mom get between us." For her, that was the obstacle. For me, it was entirely different. I'd never tell her that, though.

I began to spin her in slow, lazy circles as we swayed to the ballad. All the problems I'd seen disappeared in that moment. The music, her smell, the quiet transported me back to that boy in the shed. That boy on a bus who'd liked a girl.

With my fingers under her chin, I tipped up her head. I wiped away the single tear that had collected on her cheek. I sought out her lips and kissed her. It felt so good, that kiss. Like a culmination of all I'd wanted and desired and couldn't have for so many months. Now, though, I could have it.

Isabella needed no more urging or prompting. Her arms wound tight around my waist, pulling us together. She opened for me, giving me full access to all of her.

All those fantasies I'd had flooded my brain. Suddenly nothing mattered more than getting both of us naked. I fumbled with, but finally got my pants undone and kicked them off. My shirt was an equal challenge. When I stopped wrangling with my own clothing, I saw that Bella was free of all the pink and velour and had on nothing more than her bra and panties. Without prompting, she lay on her back on my bed.

I wasn't yet past the point of no return, but I was pretty damned close. I sat on the edge of my own bed and stroked the silk of the ponytail that spilled across my pillow.

"Are you sure about this?"

I'd have bet all of Father's money that she hadn't been unfaithful to our pledge. That she was as much a virgin as she'd been when we'd promised to be each other's firsts.

She propped herself on an elbow. Her trust in me shone through her eyes. I wanted so much to be worthy of that.

Her lids closed, then opened.

"I love you," she said.

I knew then I had to play my part. I had to make this as good as I could for her.

"God, you're so beautiful, Bella. The name, it still suits you."

With my newfound expertise, I unclasped her bra. She lifted and I tossed the scrap of pink to the floor. Instantly, I was transported back in time. We locked eyes and laughed just like we used to.

Nearly simultaneously, we shucked our underwear. She was...beautiful. I chastised myself when I compared her to Liling. As if Bella could read my mind, she traced the skin on my chest as if to bring me back to the present. To the girl in front of me. To the girl who'd loved me unwaveringly without question. Without interruption.

"I want to touch you too, Bella."

I brushed a thumb against her nipple, hard from the cold draft sneaking through the window. I weighed her breast, so much more than... No, this was Bella. I weighed her breasts in my hands, grateful that she was giving herself to me in this way. I wanted to explore more, but when her finger ran along the back of my dick, I lost it.

I molded my mouth against hers. My hands moved from her neck to her back, along her sides, on her thighs. Faster than I imagined, I was ready. I fisted my cock in my hands, pumping it, priming it for her.

Condom. Liling was on something, but I doubted Bella was.

"I'm going to get a condom, okay?" I got up and rifled through Abbott's desk until I found the string of unused foil packets. I ripped off one of the black squares. I sat on the edge of the bed again, this time rolling the latex onto myself.

She turned to me when I lay down next to her.

"I want you," she whispered.

I was glad she was ready. I didn't know how much longer I could hold out. I slid on top of her. She opened her thighs, but not nearly enough.

"More." Then, like I'd done more times in the last few months than I could count, I pushed up her leg so her foot was flat on the covers. I grasped my cock and rubbed the tip from the top to the bottom of her slit. Her hips jerked. Her teeth caught her bottom lip.

I didn't wait for a further invitation. I felt for her opening and pushed in hard.

She winced as she gasped.

"It hurts the first time, Bella. I'm sorry."

The only way through it was through it, I knew. So I kept going. I went slowly so that her body could adjust to mine.

When the pain cleared from her eyes, I didn't hold back. She was so tight. She felt *so* good. She looked amazing, her mouth half open, breath puffing against her lips, her tits bobbing in rhythm. I came harder than I had in a long time.

Bella looked confused.

"It felt too good," I explained. "I couldn't stop."

"It's okay," she said.

Wrapping my hand around the top of the condom, I pulled out. I thanked God there wasn't any blood. I hadn't wanted to hurt Bella any more than a first time had to.

"Did it rip?" she asked.

I looked closer—and saw that the tip had a tear. I wasn't used to condoms and wondered if I'd pulled it down too far. It was too late to fix it, though. Maybe Bella was on the pill. She'd obviously planned for this to happen.

"Yeah, are you okay though?" I asked.

"I'm fine."

Relief flooded through me. Thank goodness she'd planned ahead. Girls had to be smart about this kind of thing, though.

"It'll be fine," she finished.

For the second time that night, I dug through Abbott's desk until I found tissue. I think he was the only one of the three of us whose mother had raised him right. I took off what was left of the condom and jammed it in the bottom of our trash can.

Bella still lay there looking disconcerted.

"Do you have something to sleep in? You should put something on." The body that had turned me on moments before wasn't something I wanted to see anymore. Guilt gnawed at me from so many directions, I would be surprised if my digestive system could survive it.

She pulled some stuff from her duffle and shoved it on really quickly. It was lacy and black and designed for seduction. My guilt eased a bit.

"We should get some sleep. There's a big brunch tomorrow," I said. Between the beer and the sex, my eyes were drooping. I was looking forward to hours of oblivion. "You should come." I yawned. "You can meet the rest of my friends."

I didn't think she'd bother with all that. Especially with Cole being there. I hoped she'd pack and be gone before anyone met her. Before I closed my eyes, I figured out that maybe my life needed two separate parts, the New Jersey part and the Woodward Tillman part.

I pulled the chain again, this time plunging the room in near darkness. I'd figure out a way to walk back that invitation in the morning.

"What about your roommates?" Isabella asked.

"There are some overnight guest rooms for when day students stay. Or they could crash in someone else's room who's away for the weekend. Don't sweat it."

When I blinked my eyes open, watery spring sun was leaking around the sides of the window shades. I was both cold and hot at the same time. Then I remembered.

Isabella.

I turned to see her curled under the blanket dead to the world. Even with her makeup smudged dark around her eyes and her hair stiff, she looked much younger and more innocent than she tried to portray. I stroked her cheek, her lips. I couldn't believe I'd never really seen her sleep before. Maybe naps or after movies gone on too late. We'd never spent the night together, though.

It had been the fulfillment of my teenage boy fantasy. I very much wanted to put the entire experience in a box, close that box and tuck it away, like Min Li had put my baby pictures on a high and unreachable shelf in the attic.

That beer I hadn't pissed away last night pushed me out of bed. I picked up my shower kit and some clothes, jeans, a long-sleeved tee, and maroon school zip-front hoodie. Once I'd taken the world's longest piss, I hopped in the shower to rinse the smell of Isabella off me and dressed quickly.

Towel in hand, I passed Abbott in the hall.

"Tyler's girl made a big vat of hot chocolate. You should get some."

Normally, I'd have passed on the sickly sweet American drink and the backslapping testosterone-fueled boy stuff, but going back to face Isabella seemed a lot harder.

"Sure. I'll see you in there."

I detoured away from room eight toward room twelve. It was a quad with its own bathroom. I twisted the handle. Cole was already in there with some others.

"You guys up already?" I said to the group. These were not normally early risers.

"The heat in the guest rooms was off," Abbott said. He hefted his half-full mug in my direction. "Facilities wasn't working overtime to fix it so close to break and graduation."

"Broken? Sorry."

"I think they turned it off to save money. If we'd reserved it, I'm sure it would have been fine," Cole added.

"That sucks."

"You did get laid, though, right? I don't want to think we froze our balls off for nothing."

I think I was hardwired not to kiss and tell. Whether it was Chinese culture or respect for women, I couldn't tell. Instead of answering, I found my way to the big metal container and poured myself some hot chocolate from the spout into a mug turned upside down on the mini fridge.

I drank deeply like it was the best thing I'd ever had. Oddly, it kind of was. Instead of sweet, it was...it had a bite.

"Is there alcohol in this?" I sputtered.

"Rum. Kelsey borrowed this big silver whatever-it's-called thing from the dining hall. Poured in boiling water, cocoa mix, and a bottle of Jamaican rum she brought back from winter break. Like it?"

I nodded. Suddenly everything felt not only warmer but better. I finished off my first mug and poured myself a second. I looked around the room and wondered where Kelsey had gone to. It was just Tyler, Abbott, Cole, Liam from Dublin, and me.

"What's the story with the Jersey girl," Tyler asked.

"How do you..."

"She came through the common area looking for you after driving all through campus in that red car. What is that? I've never seen one."

"My father is thinking of making a go of car manufacturing in the States."

"You make it sound like he took up watercolor painting."

"Kind of. It's my grandfather's business. He's expanded it

and now wants to expand some more. He wants to be the Chinese Toyota, I think."

"Is that your car?"

"No, it's Isabella's."

"So that's her name," Tyler said appraisingly. "How does your New Jersey girlfriend have one of your father's cars. He let her borrow it to drive up to see you? Your father's pretty cool."

"What's the real story?" Cole butt in.

The liquor had loosened my tongue. "It was just a one-time thing, okay? She just showed up out of the blue since she got her license. She can barely drive. I felt bad that she'd done three hours in the car. So I did the right thing. Took her to dinner. Took her to bed. I'm hoping she gets the hint and is out of here before Liling gets wind of it at brunch." I looked at all of them, including Tyler's third roommate, who came in right at that moment. "You too. What happened with Isabella never goes outside this room. Got it."

Each one mimed some variation of zipping or locking their lips. Bro code. I'd hated it up until now when it would finally benefit me.

Kelsey, looking a little worse for wear, stumbled into the room.

"Guys!" she whisper-shouted. "Guys!"

We all stopped talking and turned in her direction. "What?" Tyler asked.

"Woody...is on his way upstairs."

"Why does a house parent go by the name of Woody?" Abbott asked, unable to stop himself from descending into giggles. From the looks of it, everyone had been indulging in a little too much "hot chocolate."

"Shhh. I need help lifting this thing. We need to dump it in the bathroom, now!"

Abbott and Tyler lifted the large metal canteen between them and rushed out of the room. Like lemmings, we all followed to make sure they made it.

They took a big swing through the bathroom and poured the contents into the shower. Brown lumps from the cocoa mix didn't go down the drain.

"We gotta do something about that."

"No, we don't. Let's just tell him that one of you has diarrhea. He'll run back downstairs faster than you can say go."

Abbott, the most persuasive of all of us, was sent to deliver the news. Like Tyler had predicted, Mr. Hopkins was back downstairs like a shot.

"How did you know?" I asked.

"He's a big old germaphobe," Liam said. "He keeps baby wipes on his coffee table. He doesn't have a baby."

"Gross," Kelsey said.

We all spilled out into the hall to get away from the sickening sweet smell of chocolate and away from evidence we had anything to do with it.

"Who was the 'round the way' girl?" Griffin, a boy who lived down the hall, asked as he came down the hall toward the bathroom. "Also, does it smell like a Godiva chocolate store exploded in there?"

"Oh, snap. She's like the very definition of 'around the way girl,'" Tyler said, snapping his fingers in emphasis.

"Nineteen-ninety called and it wants its song back," Cole responded.

"Fuck you," Tyler said. "It's true. Cole, I thought Toms River wasn't ghetto."

"Isabella is *not* Toms River," Cole responded hotly. "Got there a couple of years ago," Cole continued. "Story is that she's either a Mafia princess or daughter of Jake's housekeeper. Never got the straight scoop on that."

"Man, that's dope. I vote for housekeeper's daughter. They should have a tab for that on sultrynewcummers dot com."

"I know, right? I had to go out and kill it. Jake never fessed up that he had pussy on the premises. Now I know why he wasn't desperately trying to hook up in school," Cole said.

"Guys. C'mon," I said. That gnawing guilt was back, taking away the rum buzz I'd worked up with the spiked hot chocolate.

"What? Oh, we're sorry, man." Tyler's apology wasn't sincere. "You're the one who told us this was a one-time hookup just to get her to go home. That she wasn't the kind of girl to bring home to Mama. My dad says that's the kind of girl to hit it with early."

"Was it good practice?" Cole asked as he pushed open the bathroom door to check if the chocolate had gone down the drain.

If Isabella heard any of this, it would kill her, I thought. But she wasn't here. I had to navigate Woodward Tillman. Do my best to fit in here where kids like me had never been before. My father's position and money was the thin line between acceptance and being an outcast.

"Got my dick wet," I said.

The bathroom echoed with laughter, the tiles making it a loud cacophony against the early morning quiet.

"You guys gotta shut it." I held my finger against my lips. "She could come out in the hall at any moment."

"Gotcha, man. We're out. See you after brunch. It's not like she'll ever be back in Connecticut, anyway."

"Unless she goes to Owen," someone said, which started the howling laughter again. They all went back to Tyler's room.

I followed Tyler and helped them clean up the rest of the mess we'd made. Half an hour later, I was equal parts surprised and relieved when I pushed open the door to find the room empty.

Bella had been on the same page after all. We'd hooked up, and now we'd each go back to our regularly scheduled lives.

CHAPTER 16

FOURTEEN YEARS EARLIER...

"I'M glad you were able to come, Wu Jian." This was the nicest Min Li had ever been to me. Something about my admission to the top school in the country had changed her tune. It was as if she were silently reaping the rewards for all her supposedly great parenting.

"I really need to get back right after Christmas. I need to write a few papers and get ready for exams in January." What I said was technically true. What I wasn't saying is that spending time in Toms River had lost all its appeal years ago. Woodward Tillman had really become home, and now that home was in Cambridge.

In Massachusetts, there was no Bella or Maria Sofia. At Harvard, there were no minefields to tiptoe around or secrets to keep. School is an amazingly simple place to conduct life. I'd only been home a few hours and I was already eager to return.

"That's less than a week from now. I don't understand why there are so many weeks between the end of the

classes and the exams for the classes. Liling's schedule is
nothing like that," Min Li all but whined. What she
wanted, I'm sure, was to show me off at the club, to her
New York City friends, to Father's colleagues. That was
probably what half of tonight was about. Somehow, my
American boarding school and university cred lent them an
air of legitimacy their Chinese credentials and money
didn't.

"Liling is at USC." I pointed out the obvious.

"It's a good school."

"It does not have the weight of three hundred sixty-seven
years of tradition," I said. This...this from the woman who'd
hired tutors and had drawn up her own secondary lesson
plan when we'd moved to America because education here—
even at a prep school—wasn't enough. I'd applied and been
accepted to the oldest and most prestigious institution in the
United States. It had been my foolproof plan to get them off
my back. There was nothing better, except maybe Oxford or
the London School of Economics in England. Those had
been too far away for Father and his idea of an ongoing
mentorship in the ways of Woo DynoAutomotive. So
Harvard it had been.

"You are right. A girl doesn't need all that...tradition...not
from here, I guess. I should go check on her."

Of course Liling was here. Her mother and father had
bought her an apartment in Vancouver a few years back.
Probably had bought the one in Los Angeles as well. I hadn't
asked. I hadn't wanted to share intimacies, get closer.

Min Li and Liling's mother had a completely different
idea, though. I had no idea when I'd been summoned for this

party that Liling had already taken up residence in a guest room.

"Why don't you. I need to get dressed anyway."

"The receiving line will be promptly at eight thirty."

"Don't worry. I'll be there."

"Why is this so important?" I asked Father an hour later when we were both at the top of the stairs. I could already hear the music. Sounded like Dad had hired a harpist. The caterers were there as well. The smell of American and Chinese food wafted upstairs. A glass broke. Someone swore in Spanish.

"We're going to make an announcement."

"What?"

"We're ready to break ground for the American division of DynoAutomotive. Got the permits in place. Tax breaks and county grants in place. Six years of tax amnesty. If we start building in the spring, we'll be a fully operational factory in two years. We can move some operations here, or start with American-friendly designs. Either way, though, it will be done by the time you're done with school.

My roommates, my friends, my classmates. Most of them spent time contemplating their futures over coffee, over dining-hall food, over beer. I never joined in those discussions because I could not for the life of me think about anything but which division of Father's business I'd be working for. With that piece of the puzzle fitted in, I could cross small appliances off my list. Cars had to be better anyway.

"Those shoes?"

We both looked down at my checkered Vans.

"I'm here when I could be studying."

Father looked at his watch. "We better get down, otherwise Min Li will kill us both."

I stood behind Father and Min Li as they instituted an honest-to-goodness receiving line. I looked around at the group of workers, but I didn't see Maria. She was usually at the door greeting guests or in the kitchen managing caterers. The scene, the Christmas tree, the lights dimmed with twinkling strings everywhere took me back to how much life Isabella had brought to this house.

The first party after she'd moved in, we'd snuck down from the family room, where we'd been allowed to watch movies. First her stomach had growled. Then mine. Like little bandits, we'd skulked through the house to the kitchen. She'd put a bunch of steamed buns in her shirt and had made it upstairs undetected.

Baozi had never been my favorite, but Isabella had loved them so. I'd added a few to a cloth napkin I'd snatched from a drawer and got upstairs undetected as well. We'd eaten way too many and could barely move when her mom came up later to take her home. Every time I'd walked past a street cart when I was back in China, that smell would take me back. Now, with the party lights, it was a double whammy.

At least I wouldn't have to see her. Father had never socialized with the staff. I did not count what he did with Maria as socializing. I really hoped it was all over, but wasn't holding out a lot of hope.

It was just one of the many things I'd learned to compartmentalize, like finding out about my real mother, like pretending Min Li *was* my real mother. Like separating Liling from Isabella in my mind. All of it. Each person. Each situation went into a tiny box, shoved away in my mind. Only to be examined under the most dire of circumstances.

In a few minutes, the doorbell rang and a hired butler opened the door and started receiving guests. I nodded, shook hands, sometimes bowed—Dad had hired some Japanese engineers from Toyota—and was pleasant to every single person who walked through the door. My phone buzzed and I palmed it.

"When can u escape?" Liling had texted.

I didn't have a single second to text back. I was about to excuse myself, begging off to go to the bathroom or something, when everything left my mind.

Min Li hadn't warned me. Father hadn't warned me.

I felt her before I saw her.

What I saw was Maria Aconi walking into the house like she didn't work there. The outfit she wore looked like it cost as much as one of Min Li's. I was ninety-nine percent sure she still worked here. No one had said different. But she was walking into the door like a guest.

Maria Aconi's lean in to kiss my cheek, like...I don't know, like she was family, was odd. I'd never seen her bare shoulders, I think, nor her legs in hose and high heels.

The fact that Isabella's mother was attractive was like a punch in the gut. I'm not sure I'd ever noticed. I wish I hadn't noticed now.

Min Li's eyes were narrowed. Father's had gone wide.

What I'd *felt* was Isabella.

When I could finally look beyond Maria Aconi, there she was. All grown up. A long-sleeved black velvet dress was wrapped around her body, leaving her shoulders bare. Some kind of earrings sparkled against her neck. Her olive skin was winter pale and flawless.

Min Li, first in line, held Isabella's hand for no more than the time required not to be rude.

Her, "Lovely to see you, Isabella," could have won an Oscar for most insincere greeting ever. I had to reconsider all I'd thought I'd kept secret. Maybe she knew more than she let on. Maybe she knew her husband very well. Or maybe she was just a snob. I could only imagine the fight Mother and Father had that resulted in the help being invited guests.

More surprising than Min Li's thinly veiled attempt at civility was Isabella's response. "You as well. Hope you're enjoying the holiday season. It's good that you can come home and finally be with your family. Mr. Wu gets so lonely—"

I looked between all four of them. Maria Aconi, Father, Min Li, and Isabella. Isabella had grown fangs in the years since I'd last spent time with her. I'd been away, first at Woodward Tillman, then at Harvard.

She, on the other hand, had been here, every single day, in the thick of deception and manipulation. I was sorry for her because the exposure had made her something she hadn't been when she'd moved in—unkind.

Father cupped his large hands around Isabella's shoulders and moved her out of Min Li's reach. "Isabella!" His voice was too loud, as if he could silence any questions someone may have had. "I hear you've applied to Owen. Good for you. Two Ivy Leaguers in the family can't be a bad thing."

Owen? I tilted my head slightly and looked at the girl

who was once my best friend in a completely different light. She'd applied to the second-most prestigious university in America. It's not like I'd believed everything Min Li had said, but I'd expected her to maybe go to Ramapo or one of those public schools in Jersey no one had ever heard of. Rutgers, if she really pulled it together.

But Owen, our main rival? Probably her reach school.

"Bella," I said. I used the nickname to knock her off-kilter. She couldn't hide from me. I could see in her eyes that she still carried a torch for me. My ego took a little boost at that one. Her eyes locked with mine again and she almost fell off her mile-high heels. I put both arms around her waist and braced my hands against her back.

She jumped back like I'd shocked her with a thousand volts of electricity.

She slipped through my arms like smoke, and I turned away, ready to greet the next in the line of guests.

Liling swept through the crowd in a long-sleeve long silk dress. The red color was almost subtle. Her lipstick was not. Men of every age were following her through the room with their eyes.

"Nǚshì Li," Liling started, her honorifics in place as they always were with my parents. "Would you mind if I steal Wu Jian away for a minute?"

"Go. Us older generation can handle the door," my father said, excusing us.

Sometimes Liling was like magic. She asked and Mother and Father would bend over backwards to give it to her. When I'd asked to skip the ridiculous receiving line, I'd been on the business end of a twenty-minute lecture on the importance of Chinese tradition, loyalty, and what it means to succeed in corporate America.

Not giving my parents a chance to change their minds, I guided Liling over toward the baby grand piano. There, we got drinks from a passing waiter and rested in the curve of the glossy black wood.

"How long do we have to stay?" Liling asked.

"Why? What did you have in mind?" I asked, relieved to have a break from hosting duties.

"There's a little jazz bar I heard about in some place called Avon-by-the-Sea that we should check out."

"Meet me by the garage in thirty minutes," I said. "I have a couple of things I have to do. Obligations. Family stuff. But let's separate. That way, no one is suspicious."

Ninety-nine percent of the time, Liling was accommodating.

I asked.

She did.

The look in her eyes was anything but acquiescent. It had a look a bit like one of the feral cats that Bella and I had found on the property not too long after the discovery of the rats in the shed.

"Who was that girl?"

"What girl?" I asked, as if I had zero idea who she was talking about. She wasn't fooled.

"The one in the black velvet dress who practically fell all over you."

"Oh, you mean Isabella?" I feigned mild indifference.

"Yes. Isabella."

"Daughter of the housekeeper. They live in a cottage on the property."

"How old is she?"

"Still in high school," I said, like Bella was sixteen and not a fully legal eighteen, free to do what she wanted with whom.

"Something about that name sounds familiar." Liling cocked her head. "But I've never seen her before. How close are the two of you?"

"Not very," I lied. "It's a big property. She was just a kid when they got here." I shrugged for effect.

"Okay." She looked appeased. Bullet dodged. "Let's meet at nine fifteen." She glided away in her dress and promptly found a group of older Chinese gentlemen to befriend. They welcomed her like a long-lost daughter.

The minute her eyes had drifted from me to pay full attention to the conversation with her latest groupies, I backed away from the side of the room Liling was on. Instead, I tried to retrace Bella's steps from the time she'd left the line until she seemed to slip from the crowd.

Nearly every woman was wearing black. So many had dark hair. It took longer than it should, but I spotted her. She was a couple of steps in front of a guy I recognized from the club. He was probably a year older than me. Had gone to prep school at Exeter if my memory was right. He was at Cornell now...no, Dartmouth. I remember Coleton being a little envious of this guy, even though Cole had gotten into Princeton as a legacy.

Todd. The guy's name was Todd. He had two glasses of whiskey in his hands. Isabella was opening the door to the family room. The informal one only for family that Bella and I had hung out in so many times.

My feet were moving before my brain could think better of it. They hadn't thought to close the door all the way. Faint light formed a small halo under the door.

I inched closer until the indistinct murmur of voices in the beginning dance of the human mating ritual became clearer.

"I could turn it up, but the wallpaper may blind us," Bella whispered.

Their shared laughter went straight to my gut. I couldn't tell if it was embarrassment at Min Li's decorating choices or the fact that Isabella was sharing her husky laugh with someone who wasn't me. It didn't take much to create a picture in my mind's eye. Bella pulling bands or pins from her hair, the silk falling heavily on her shoulder, over one eye. Todd leaning closer to brush that hair over her shoulder or behind her ear to get a better look at her face, the curve of her neck.

It was what I'd have done. What I'd wanted to do more times than I can remember. What I'd never had the guts to do.

"Dartmouth's in New Hampshire, right?" Isabella was asking.

Even without the benefit of sight, I knew Todd was preening like a bird during mating season. I'd seen him do it when one girl or another would compliment his tennis serve or golf swing.

"Hanover," he said, like it was Jerusalem or the Temple of Heaven. "Colder than a witch's tit this time of year."

Isabella's voice got throatier, sexier. "Maybe I'd be warm if I had one of those long green-and-white striped scarves," she said. I heard her pause to take a sip of the drink Todd had gotten for her.

"I don't know if you'd be warm, but you'd be incredibly beautiful," he said.

My God, did he think that would work? It was the most clichéd thing I'd heard outside a bar in forever.

The whisky had turned Isabella from high school senior to sexy siren. "You didn't have to say that."

"But it's true. The incoming freshmen at Owen are going to be incredibly lucky."

It got unnervingly quiet after that. Wool and velvet shifted against the sofa cushion.

"Cold?" Todd's voice was deep.

"Warming up." Isabella's bordered on the indecent.

The half-moon of light disappeared. There were no more words after that. Only the sound of fabric shifting and heavy breathing coming from the room.

I needed to walk away. Join the party. Schmooze with my father's managers. Introduce Liling to people from the club. Eat some of the food that had the flavors of home that I missed so much.

I didn't do any of that. Instead, I pushed into the family room and flicked the switch that lit the overhead light. The chandelier threw everything into stark relief.

"Bella."

Surprise widened Isabella's eyes only a millimeter before she got back her composure.

"If you'll excuse us, Jake. Todd was telling me a bit about his time at Dartmouth."

I didn't look at her. I couldn't. Instead, I turned toward Todd. "Sheridan."

Todd hoisted Isabella from him. My eyes went to her then. She was fully dressed. He hadn't touched or seen... anything. I had been so busy concentrating on Isabella's state of undress, that I hadn't heard anyone behind me.

Min Li's "Wu Jian" grated on every nerve of my body. "You need to come out to the living room," she started. The "and leave that girl the hell alone" went unsaid. "There are some people your father wants you to meet."

I couldn't be moved. My feet stuck to the floor as if glue were keeping my Vans there. "I need to talk to Isabella."

Min Li continued in English. No doubt out of deference to Todd. She'd rarely extended Isabella that courtesy.

"This is the last time I'm going to tell you to leave this girl alone," she barked. "Let her trap another rich man."

Mother stalked from the room. Like a whipped puppy, I followed her. I was surprised when Todd brought up the rear. My take on him had been right. He was not a stand-up guy who was deserving of Isabella's attention.

"You should have stuck up for her in there," I threw over my shoulder, sotto voce.

He lifted and dropped a shoulder, all the while putting his tuxedo back together.

Todd peeled off when we got back to the main hall.

"Wu Jian. How many times—"

"It's been enough times, Mother. I went in there to break

it up. I didn't want this party turning into something that might scandalize Father's company." The lie was twisted and tortured, but she nodded.

Then we both turned as a huge, discordant chord filled the room. I looked to see Isabella's hands coming up from the baby grand piano keys. She swayed a little before she got steady on her feet. The party went from boisterous to nearly silent in a heartbeat.

"I have an announcement," she said.

I racked my brain trying to figure out what in the hell Isabella had to say to a crowd of my parents' acquaintances. She couldn't know a single person from the party outside the Perezes, who were huddling in a corner watching the festivities like it were a movie.

Before she could get off her chest whatever was burdening her, Father grabbed her arm in a viselike grip and steered her across the room.

"That girl." My mother shook her head.

"Who was that?" Liling asked, materializing at my side.

"That's our housekeeper's daughter," Min Li hissed under her breath in Mandarin. She made no attempt to hide her contempt in our native language.

"Why is she even at the party?" Liling inquired. It would never have been done in China.

"Feng Wu is on some American egalitarianism thing. He was talking about how in this country everyone is equal and needs to be treated that way. How our employees will be more loyal if we come down to their level. I think it's nonsense, but it was just this one night. Not worth the fight."

Min Li was more candid with Liling than she'd ever been

with me. Or maybe it was the alcohol. Her cheeks were pretty red and her eyes were a little bit glassy.

"Jake, let's go." Liling took my hand in hers. "Mrs. Li. I'm sorry about this. I wanted to show Jake something. We'll be back soon."

Min Li didn't even blink before she nodded in acquiescence.

Liling was leading me toward the stairs instead of outside.

"What about the jazz club?" I wanted to be anywhere but here within Isabella's orbit.

"We need to talk first." Her grip was as firm as a vise. I didn't protest. My parents had already suffered one scene. They didn't need another.

In a few minutes, we were in her guest bedroom. Clothes were everywhere, as if her suitcase had exploded rather than been unpacked when she got here.

"Who is that girl?"

I feigned ignorance trying to swallow the panic that was threatening to choke me. Except for the few days after Bella's Tillman visit, I hadn't worried about Liling and Isabella finding out about each other. My housemates had kept quiet and I'd moved on with Liling as if nothing had happened. And when I'd gone east and her west it had been a natural end to our relationship. An easy way to say goodbye to something that had been a kind of stand-in for something else.

"Sorry?"

"Don't play dumb, Wu Jian. Jake Wu. Who was the girl banging on the piano? The one who upset your mother? The one who fell all over you at the door. This girl is getting a lot of attention for someone who isn't important."

"She's who Mother said. She's the housekeeper's daughter."

"I have housekeepers. In the Vancouver house. In the Los Angeles house. In the Shanghai house. Even the Shamian house has a housekeeper. I've never met a single daughter, or son, for that matter, of any of them."

"She lives in one of the back houses."

"Okay. And?"

"We...Isabella and I were close friends at one time."

As if the life had gone out of her legs suddenly, heaps of red silk whooshed as Liling's butt hit the bed covers.

"You loved her. You were in love with her. Are you still in love with her?"

"No...it's not like that...no."

"For years I've been trying to get you to love me. Trying to figure out why you *didn't* love me. Trying to figure out why I wasn't enough. I had no idea that it was only because I wasn't some other girl. Min Li didn't even tell me. *You* certainly didn't."

"That's not...it's not—"

"No, it is exactly that. You loved or still love someone else. That girl has a hold on your heart. She takes up so much that there's no space for anyone else. I've been competing with a real live girl I never knew about!"

"I'm sorry. She's not in my life. I haven't seen her in years."

"But she's in your *heart*, Wu Jian. You may not admit it to yourself. But your parents know. Your heart knows. It's why you left me alone to be pawed at by your father's drunk employees. It's what probably had you chasing her down into some corner."

"She was in a corner with someone else, actually."

"How did that make you feel?"

"I...uh...I didn't want Todd Sheridan taking advantage of her. He's not...he's not a stand-up guy," I said borrowing a New Jersyism.

"That girl looks like no one has *ever* taken advantage of her. She looks like she one hundred percent knows what she's doing. It's *me* who has gotten the short end of the stick."

She stood and started bunching clothes in the middle of the king-size bed.

"What are you doing?"

"Packing. Leaving. You don't want me. I need to find someone who does, Jake. I'm done chasing you. I'm done playing a game where no one gave me the rules."

"But...I love you, Lily...Liling." I knew it wasn't true the minute the words formed on my lips and pushed past them. It came out because I felt awful for using Liling. For being someone who couldn't ever do the right thing.

"You've said that before, Jake. Wu Jian. You've said it a hundred times when we were in bed together. And ninety-nine of those times I believed it. This time, I know it's something you're saying to make yourself feel better. For using me. For wasting my time. Have a merry Christmas and happy New Year."

"I...uh..."

"Get out, Wu Jian! I can't look at you right now. What I see on your face is too humiliating to bear."

Like a coward, I walked out the door. Closed it softly behind me. For the first time in a long time, I regretted what I'd done.

I couldn't think of a single way I could go back and fix it. Fix Bella who was hurt and broken. Fix Liling's heart which I'd smashed into a million pieces by making one colossal mistake after another because being with her had been easier than being without her.

Min Li would never have Jägermeister at this party. But I was sure there was something behind the bar that could make this all go away. Then when I could, I'd slip away, back to Cambridge where I didn't have to deal with any of this... mess...we'd all made.

CHAPTER 17

THIRTEEN YEARS EARLIER...

MY DORM ROOM at Kirkland House wasn't much different than the one I'd had at Woodward Tillman. Except I didn't have to share a bathroom with everyone, only the two other guys I roomed with. They shared the larger room, I had the smaller one to myself. The couch in the common room was older than the one we'd had at Woodward, but so was the school.

I paced from one end of the small room to the other. I'd worry about wearing a pattern in the oak floor, except that had already been done by the hundreds of occupants before me in the last seventy-three years.

I flung the door open at the first knock.

"Liling. It's so good to see you," I said.

She rolled a small suitcase into the common room. I took it from her and steered it toward my bedroom.

"It's a lot different than I thought," Liling said, following me farther inside. She stood awkwardly in the room that served as both my bedroom and study area.

"It's Harvard. They don't need to impress," I said.

Gingerly, as if she were going to get a splinter or be infected by some kind of mold spores, Liling arranged herself on my wooden desk chair. It was ugly, oak, and utilitarian.

"Are you hungry? There's the dining room, of course. But there's a lot to eat in Cambridge. A few of us love this really good Cape Verdean place in Dorchester. We could take the T." I looked at her face, trying to gauge her feelings. I'd already run out of small talk.

"I didn't come all the way to Massachusetts to eat, Wu Jian."

She didn't want small talk either. That left only the hard stuff. I wasn't ready to face the hard stuff. I only wanted to go back to how things had been when they were easy. Before the ghost of Isabella had come between us.

"But you have to eat, right? You have to be hungry. It's a long ride up here from New Jersey," I pressed. If we had food between us, something to do with our hands, we could get to the reconciling part. The apology part.

"Your dad had a driver bring me."

"Takeout. I could do that. We get pizza all the time. There's even a half-decent Chinese place that delivers. I could get your favorite, Lion's head meatballs."

"That sounds fine," she said. "Order it so we can stop talking about food."

I made a call on my cell. Delivery was promised in less than a half hour. The restaurant lived up to its promise and knocked on the door in fifteen minutes flat.

It felt like everything came more quickly during reading period when everyone was hunkered down like we were weathering a blizzard, and not just the imminent onslaught of first semester exams. We'd filled the time talking about every Chinese person we had in common, but I was grateful when I had a plastic bag to untie and chopsticks to wield in place of talking.

I cleared off my desk and arranged the food in the most attractive way possible.

Liling took one of the chairs I'd brought with me from New Jersey. I picked the uncomfortable one supplied by the school.

"I want to apologize," I said after a few bites. I lowered my bamboo chopsticks and looked her in the eye for the first time since she'd been here.

"For what?"

Liling was not going to make this easy by any means.

"For that incident at the Christmas party. I don't know what came over me."

"You don't? You have no idea what made you follow your housekeeper's daughter to a dark room and barge in on her... how do the Americans say it...hooking up with some Dartmouth guy?"

"I think it's time I tell you the truth."

"I should hope so." She rested her chopsticks as well. Looked at me with expectation all over her face.

My sigh was long. I'd already lost one woman. I didn't want to lose the second. The only one who'd loved me almost unconditionally. I think I needed a woman like Liling by my side. Someone to help me weather all the hard things that were going to come after when I started working in Father's business full-time.

"Isabella moved in six years ago. Father hired her mother to be our housekeeper. She lived...*lives* in the guesthouse behind ours. Another family, the caretakers, they live in another house in the back. We...became friends when we were in middle school together."

"Middle school?"

"We were both new. Kind of became friends out of necessity. They weren't nice to new kids."

"Middle school friends."

"Isabella and I were friends, kind of like you and me. Instead of sharing manga, though, we played video games. Watched movies. Stuff like that."

"Min Li let you play video games?"

"No, of course not. It was as prohibited as the manga."

"Video game buddies?"

Liling summarized every part of my history with Bella as if she could make sense of it all. I'd never even made sense of it.

"When we were like fifteen, we kissed. It didn't go anywhere. It was right before I saw you in Shanghai, before I started that winter at Woodward Tillman."

"I never did get why you had to come to Shanghai before Christmas. Why you started Tillman in the middle of the year."

There were some family secrets that were too mortifying to discuss. That one big issue, I wasn't ready to share. Didn't know if I'd ever be. It was probably what had bonded me to Isabella. Not young love, but maybe shared trauma.

"It's a family issue. I...it had nothing to do with Isabella."

I thanked goodness she was Chinese. An American girl

would have poked holes in that excuse, probed it to death. I'd seen it time and again in relationships here.

"I understand, Wu Jian. Family issues. They're always there. But I'm still not understanding what happened."

For a long moment, I wavered. What was best—compassionate lie or brutal truth? My head told me truth. My heart, compassion.

"I don't have those kinds of feelings for Isabella anymore. Not in years. Todd Sheridan, though. That guy she went into the family room with. He's a player. He has a reputation at the club for pulling any willing girl into an empty room or a closet or whatever and deflowering her. It's kind of a sport with him. Isabella's mother, Maria? She's a devout Catholic. I didn't want my father's guest to be responsible for something that we could all regret. Not on our property, at least. We'd lose face for sure."

"You weren't jealous?"

It was time for another compassionate lie. It had always been Bella. Except for that moment at Woodward Tillman when I'd been crazy off my ass with misplaced shame, it would probably always be Bella.

But I wasn't my father. I was not going to let emotions rule me. Smart people made choices. Men who were no longer boys made smart choices. Liling was that smart choice. If I tried hard enough with her, I could push Bella farther and farther into the past. Fulfill the destiny that had been laid out before me.

"No, just concerned. Just because I don't like her anymore doesn't mean I wish anything bad to happen to her."

"Why did you stop liking her?"

"It was a childhood crush. Not my first, but just a crush."

"Who was your first?"

"I think you know the answer."

"Really? Who? Someone we went to school with in Shanghai?"

"Very much a girl I went to school with there. She's about your height. Same hair. I used to buy manga with her."

"It's me?" Despite my dead-on description, Liling's face was awash in uncertainty.

"Of course it was you," I said. It was almost the truth. She had stirred something in me during those early days when just the thought of someone of the female persuasion was enough to make me hard.

"Why didn't you ever tell me?"

"It's embarrassing. I wanted you to love the man who loves you now, not the boy who loved you then."

"Do you? Love me? This is the first time you've said it when we weren't...you know...doing it."

"Of course, Liling. I'm sorry if things have been a little distant, off, between us. It's been hard studying here, working for Father in between. Trying to live up to everyone's expectations."

"You could have talked to me. I know how it is."

I didn't think that was exactly true. I was expected to take over my father's business. Support my family and my future wife. She was expected to go to school, be smart. Look pretty. She took her studies pretty seriously, though. Said she was going to be the right hand to her father, so I didn't say what I really thought, what would likely be the truth going forward, that us being together would be expedient. A perfect business arrangement like those that had gone on in families for thousands of years in Asia, in Europe, in all the places where legacies mattered.

Instead, I put down my chopsticks, pushed aside the food, lifted her hand and guided her to my bed. I'd gotten a second twin from storage, pushed them together and had made a king in the room. It was my one concession to comfort.

Gently, I laid her on the bed. The duvet was the right kind this time, blue and green shiny cotton over a down insert. With every kiss, I vowed to do this relationship right this time. With every caress, I committed to making this work.

Bella wasn't right for me. Not now. Liling was perfect in so many ways. I just had to try hard enough to make her perfect for *me*.

I hated that Min Li was right. I'd tried living differently. Coloring outside the lines and it had ended in disaster. My father was doing it now and he was making everyone miserable. There were so many good things about Liling. The best was that she loved me. She'd make a loyal and faithful wife one day.

If we married, it would be the ultimate merger of families. That's what marriage had been for centuries and probably would be for years to come.

I was growing up. No one got everything they wanted. I was grateful to have the love of a good woman. Big crazy beautiful love stories, those—those were for everybody else.

CHAPTER 18

SEVEN YEARS EARLIER...

"THIS WEATHER," I said as I brushed water from my over-coat in the vestibule of the Eighteenth Street bar. I stepped in behind Cole. To say the place wasn't what I expected was an understatement. People were drinking out of ceramic coconut mugs and there were honest-to-God paper umbrellas in some drinks. It was like I'd stepped into the tackiest Chinese restaurant in New York City's Chinatown.

"We can dry off before we go to that Ivy thing later," Cole said.

"Are we in the right place?" I asked.

"Bro. I wouldn't steer you wrong. This upstairs part is for tourists and middle managers. Follow me, dude." I did follow Cole. With the confidence of a rich scion, he strode through the bar toward the back. A small sign read, "The Franklin Mortgage & Investment Company." He turned a handle and started down steep stairs. I followed as the heavy wood door shut behind me, throwing the steps into semi-darkness.

Down at the bottom, though, was the real bar.

"The Franklin Mortgage & Investment Company?"

"The name of this place during prohibition, dude. That top part was added later. Down here is where the real bar was in the late twenties."

Prohibition was one of those American things I didn't understand. The culture seemed to bounce between puritanism when it came to sex and outright indulgence when it came to violence. Booze always walked a line between blue laws where it couldn't be sold on Sundays and half-naked women pushing beer on the same Sundays during football games.

I nodded my head like I'd learned years earlier. My "cool" was sufficient to show that I was onboard with whatever.

Cole raised his hand and a waiter materialized in seconds.

"Jack and Coke."

"Old Fashioned," I said. It had taken me a couple of years and some deep soul searching via Google to pick a go-to drink. Had to be macho enough to not get any blowback from guys, but palatable enough to drink. This one had some sugar in it to chase away the terrible taste of bourbon. But it was as American as apple pie, so I went with it.

When the drinks came, Cole lifted his for a toast. I mimicked him.

"To our final semester," he said. I nodded, clinked his glass, and took a long sip. It helped put me in the frame of mind to deal with Cole. After all these years, I guess we were friends. He'd gone to Princeton, his father's alma mater, while I'd gone to school in Cambridge. We'd met back up at Wharton and now we were doing this final project together.

"You wanted to talk about school?" I asked. Cole never wanted to talk about school. Drinking. Traveling. Getting girls to sleep with him, yes. School, never.

"We're in Managing the Established Enterprise together this semester," he said.

We'd just finished our first week of the spring term. It was only the second class we'd had together though. The sixteen-hundred-plus students in our program dwarfed both the law school and medical school classes, which were tiny by comparison. Those programs bred incestuous closeness. This one bred outsized competition.

"The bulk of our grade is a team project," he started. "I think that we should start working on it together. My dad's equity firm has just become the majority stockholder in Safetri."

I blinked. I could feel my eyes open and shut. Father had mentioned this in passing over dinner during the holiday break, but I hadn't thought much about it. He'd tried to impress upon me the importance of keeping up ties with Coleton. How there could be a huge advantage to having an inside connection with Safetri.

Dad's plant was humming along, selling about one hundred thousand units a year, similar to what Porsche and Range Rover were doing. But without the high luxury markup those brands enjoyed, the profit margins were slim. One of the biggest costs, thanks to endless new regulations from the National Highway Traffic Safety Administration, was safety systems—airbags and seat belts.

Cole's dad's new business was just that—airbags and seat belts. A favorable contract could net dad millions, raise DynoAutomotive's profit margin from slim to healthy.

I took another sip of my drink and scooted my chair forward just enough to eliminate some of the bar noise around us.

"Your dad's okay with that?"

"More than okay. He really wants me to come on board in the fall. Obviously Safetri needs to have the fat cut so it can be sold at a profit. But we'll need a good handle on what can stay and what can go."

"Sounds good," I said. What I really wanted to know was, why me. I poked around my head for the best way to ask that question. "Think I'd be a good fit because of my father?"

He nodded. "Cars are not sexy unless you're Elon Musk. Who knows if that thing will ever get off the ground? Until then, people still need cars. Everyone in our class is into spinning out a dot com they can take public in five years and retire as billionaires. That's cute, but the real money has been and always will be in consumer goods. The Chinese get that. I get that. Can I count on you?"

I nodded. It probably didn't hurt that I was in the top of my class at Wharton and, from the rumors of Cole's partying and other exploits, he was probably near the bottom. But I had to do the work anyway for the grade. Father would be proud once I told him.

"Where is Lily these days?" he asked after he'd waved over a second round of drinks. I was banking on a cold walk across the Schuylkill River to sober me up because these were strong. I'm guessing the drinks in the tiki lounge upstairs were more on the fruity side.

"At Owen."

"Really. Doing what?"

"School of Drama."

"She wants to act now? I thought she wanted to be in television?"

"She does. It's playwriting. It's the classical education that she wants to bring back to China."

"Right. Her dad owns a network there."

"Red Dragon Television. I think she wants to bring the scripted thing home."

"So like the *Sopranos* or *The Wire*."

"Something like that."

"You still hitting it?"

"We...we took kind of a break while she was in LA and I was in Cambridge." It wasn't a mistruth. Liling was always an option. It had been hard trying to do the long-distance thing. Every time I saw her, I worried that she'd figure out my heart wasn't in it. We'd made an agreement to keep our relationship on the back burner...kind of like it was on simmer.

If either of us found someone else, then we'd agreed to have a longer talk. I was very proud of the very adult way we were handling things.

"You, Jake...you always had a lot more action than you let on. Lily and Isabella. Damn...remember her? She was something to look at, but once she opened that mouth, it scared the shit out of most guys."

I wanted to defend the girl who'd been my best friend

and maybe even my first love. But I didn't have the words to explain our very complicated situation.

"The law school is mostly women. The medical school, too. We didn't luck out at Wharton," I said.

"Man, it's a total sausage factory. Thank God this school hasn't banned sororities. Some of the guys and I have been doing parties there on the weekend. You should come, unless you've got another secret woman up your sleeve."

I didn't answer out loud. Just nodded and finished up my second drink. The idea of dating eighteen-year-old girls left me cold. There wasn't a girl worth that amount of drama. And throw in a sorority full of other girls who would just throw gas on a fire, no way.

I'd be back in China in a few months anyway.

"You ready to do that Ivy alumni thing?" I asked. If he wasn't, I'd happily get on my way back to my apartment.

"It's around the corner. Let's go. Ivy girls are sometimes the most desperate. Especially if you add in Seven Sisters graduates. They're ready to hook up in hopes that they get a ring out of it."

I let Cole pay the tab and slipped on my overcoat. The suits we were wearing would probably be overkill, but we'd both done the new semester faculty meet-and-greet before this. That wasn't an occasion for jeans even in today's business casual world.

We slogged the couple of blocks to another historic building. This one housed apartments and a bar inside. I squinted through the precipitation at the sign above the uniformed doorman. I think I'd looked at an apartment here, but had picked something on the other side of the river, closer to school.

We weren't three feet past the coat check when dark green drinks were thrust into our hands.

"It's called The Ivy," a girl who'd had far too many said. "Special for tonight. Drink up!"

Cole downed his and put the glass on the corner of the bar. I sipped it. Sweet, sour. Like a Manhattan with green dye. When no one was looking, I abandoned it. I was here to work. I hadn't gone to two different Ivy League schools just for the education. I'd done it because Father had always drilled into me it was who you knew that was nearly as important as what. It was certainly true in China. He'd schmoozed the right people in the Party and had gotten the necessary permits and concessions for his businesses.

"Have you met the guys from the Tiger Inn? Let me introduce you," Cole said. I'd learned years earlier that the Tiger Inn was one of Princeton's private eating clubs. Part of that non-egalitarian America no one talked about.

There was a lot of handshaking and talk about what our fathers did. When people first met me, they always thought I was some non-English-speaking math or science major. When they found out my father was just like theirs, only Chinese, I was usually accepted into their circles immediately. Like my father wanted to do business in America, most of their fathers wanted a connection in China. They were all relationships of convenience, though I had developed true affection for a number of the guys. Maybe even Cole. He certainly wasn't the bully I'd met in Toms River.

"Cole," a female voice snapped.

The four of us stopped talking so he could address whomever had called his name. Then I continued. "So we're not going in the hybrid or electric direction. Too expensive to manufacture without a solid customer base. We're going a little more downscale like the Korean manufacturers. Our customers are mostly the budget-conscious coastal consumer," I explained.

"That sweet ride you drive isn't exactly downscale," one of Cole's friends said. He was at the law school. We'd met in passing in the parking lot before some graduate school function off campus.

"I have one from China. Different market. I'm not sure who's making billionaires faster, China or Silicon Valley, but our market there is more upscale."

I felt a tug on the sleeve of my suit jacket from Cole. It was a subtle message that someone of interest was in our purview. I turned expecting another law school or finance guy.

It was none other than Isabella.

Some part of me knew she was here in this historic city. Father had mentioned that she'd come here after a year in New York. She looked amazing in some fitted black-and-white checked dress. The neckline showed just a bit of the top of her boobs.

Despite the drinks, despite all of the time passed, her dark hair and searching brown eyes stirred something both in my belly and in my pants. Neither feeling was exactly welcome. I'd thought time and distance and Liling had neutralized my feelings for her. It was like a kick in the head to find out none of that or the awful green drink had worked.

"Hey, man, guess who's here? POTP." This time a back-slap accompanied Cole's words.

"POTP," the woman with Priscilla handwritten on a name tag stuck to her chest questioned. "You're Jake?" She bent forward and squinted to read the tag I'd attached to my own lapel, where I'd written my name and school, as directed by the little sign on the table just past the coat check.

"Wellesley," Priscilla announced, taking first Cole's then my hand in a firm handshake. "Just a Seven Sister school, but with the rule change, here I am! You guys went to Harvard and Princeton. Wow. Where are you from, Jake? Isabella and Cole are from Toms River."

While Priscilla was talking, I saw Isabella's eyes go flat. When her friend ran out of breath, she said, "As a matter of fact, Jake was my next-door neighbor. POTP is 'pussy on the premises.' It's Cole's nickname for me, though maybe it should have been Jake's. Now, if you'll excuse me..."

Without so much as a backward glance for any of us, she turned on her little suede shoes and stalked toward the back of the bar.

"Aw, man, she used to be a good sport," Cole said.

Priscilla didn't say that we were assholes out loud, but her demeanor could have shouted it. Her lips formed into a thin line. She turned from us without comment.

"Those Seven Sisters girls never have a sense of humor," one of Cole's friends said.

Maybe because there hadn't been anything funny, I thought. I didn't say it because I wasn't changing anyone's mind today. Instead, I followed Priscilla. She talked to

Isabella, who disappeared through a back door. When she finally came back inside the bar proper, I cornered her.

"Look, I'm sorry about what happened back there. We all grew up together and it's complicated."

"Complicated? She went to Owen and the first words out of your friend's mouth are slut-shaming her. Whichever one of you slept with her should be ashamed, too. She wasn't in bed by herself, though she probably should have been."

"I'm really sorry. It was totally inappropriate. Uncalled for. Does she live here?"

"Am I going to need to get security involved?"

"No. No. Look, we were more than neighbors. She was... my first girlfriend, okay? Do you have her apartment number? I'd really like to go upstairs and apologize."

"Seriously? You're going to apologize?"

"For Cole. It wasn't me who said that. She embarrassed him when we were in middle school and he never got over it."

"Wow. Middle school. Seriously? That *is* complicated. She's in suite eleven oh two. If you can get that doorman to let you up."

That doorman wasn't a problem. I kept my Ivy League club badge firmly affixed to my custom gray wool suit and pled my case. Julius, as his name tag read, was swiping me up before I could finish my sob story.

I banged on the door even though I had no idea what I was going to say when she answered.

When the door opened, Isabella was there. The only difference between downstairs and now was that she was in stocking feet, the sheer fabric making a weird webbing across her toes. I was out of words in any language.

"Bella..."

She didn't say anything, but stepped back. I took the movement as an invitation and walked into the penthouse apartment, dropped my bag like I was going to stay a while.

The first thing I noticed was her view of Rittenhouse Square. It was an amazing apartment for a girl a few years out of college. I was trying to put together that puzzle when I noticed the second thing.

"I'm sorry, I didn't know—" I stopped mid-thought.

Isabella wasn't alone. She was there with a man Father's age. He was tall and looked nothing like I imagined her father would look like, but genetics were a funny thing.

I was suddenly glad for her that she'd reunited with him in Philly. Maybe that's why she'd come here. I could see how it wouldn't be the kind of thing she'd have mentioned to her mother, given the circumstances surrounding that divorce. I'd always been jealous that her parents had at least called it a day and not held on like mine.

Isabella titled her head. She gave me the oddest look, then sighed heavily.

"Jake. Meet Daniel Van Dijk," she said. "Daniel. This is Jake Wu."

So this wasn't Mr. Aconi. Who in the hell was this guy?

I overcame my momentary shock and extended my hand like I'd been taught. He came forward and shook. Solid gold cuff links winked in the room's light. His suit, light gray to my dark, was clearly bespoke. Probably British from the looks of it. By all accounts, this man had money. Maybe he was some kind of Ivy alumni. The meeting was for under thirties, but maybe there was some other meeting.

"Jake Wu? The one from Toms River? The one your mom worked for?" Daniel asked Isabella, his eyebrows moving up in surprise.

How did he know who I was if I didn't know *him*? I wished to God I hadn't had those two and a half drinks, because my brain was moving in slow motion. I could not put two and two together even though the numbers were right here in front of me.

"Yes, Daniel. That Jake Wu. He was just downstairs at the bar. I left when his friend referred to me as 'pussy on the premises.'"

Daniel's face went purple. "And you have the audacity—"

Clearly he was on Isabella's side.

I winced before I could declare that I was on her side also. My stomach plummeted to my toes. Out loud, in a room that wasn't as dark as a bar, it sounded horrible. It sounded like Priscilla had said, a man slut-shaming a woman. I didn't know if an apology was enough. I'd need to grovel to get her to understand that I didn't mean it. It wasn't my fault, but I would apologize for all of mankind for its horrible assumptions about women if that's what it took.

I cut Daniel off before he lost his temper. A fist fight with a senior citizen was the last thing I wanted.

"I'm here to apologize." I took another step into the room. "I can't believe Cole said that. It's out of character—"

"Oh, for fuck's sake, that's the biggest lie you've probably ever told," Isabella said.

I swallowed because if I didn't, I was going to throw up. It had been a secret. It had been my most shameful and cowardly moment in the eleven long years we'd known each other. Under pain of death, I'd never have told anyone. But she knew. All this time, she'd known.

Any Chinese stoicism I had disappeared in a heartbeat. My face was a tell-all.

"Cole called me that during that spring at Woodward Tillman. I very distinctly remember all your friends laughing —and you not doing a single thing to defend my honor."

I wanted to disappear. It was the first time I'd been faced with something so awful, so regretful. So unforgivable.

"You heard that?" My voice squeaked so hard on the last word that I knew I wasn't fooling anyone.

Right then, I knew I was nothing like my father. He'd have denied it so smoothly that any accuser would have been second-guessing herself right at this moment and not looking like Bella. Like she was going to cry and crumple into herself as she relived that long-ago humiliation.

"I was in the bathroom. I'm not hard of hearing, though. I would have probably heard it from your room."

Daniel took in air or something that made him bigger and taller. He took some more steps until he was closing in on Bella and me. Despite his age, I knew what that posture was saying. "I could take you." I had not come up here looking for a fight.

"I think an apology is in order," he demanded.

"I *am* sorry, Bella. He's an ass. Always has been," I said.

"So were you for saying what you said." Isabella shook her head. Then she asked the only logical question, "If he's such an ass, why are you hanging out with him?"

"We're working on a marketing project." The excuse sounded lame even to my own ears.

"That's why you're at a bar drinking and socializing? Because you're working on a project?"

I was hanging out with a guy who was probably a misogynistic bully, although he was nicer to me nowadays, because we were working on a school project. It sounded downright awful, downright inexcusable.

"His dad's company designs and manufactures auto-safety systems. Dad thinks having him as a friend would be advantageous," I admitted. My bottom line with Cole was money, not morality. I wanted to explain that if we only did business with those with scruples, there'd be no business done. How many strip clubs and men-only clubs was business done in?

"Advantageous. That's why he's still married to your mom, right? Because access to her family's money is advantageous. You Wus love to take *advantage*..."

I could feel heat creeping up my face, and that hardly ever happened.

My protest was weak. "It's not—"

"Yes, it is exactly. I heard your apology, so if you'll excuse me..."

There wasn't a single thing I could do to save this conversation. I'd see her again. Maybe work out how to apologize. Our parents practically lived together, so neither one of us would ever totally be out of the other's orbit.

I picked up my bag that I'd dropped by the door. Now was the time to make that walk home. I glanced over my shoulder through the windows. The sleet looked like it had stopped. At least I wouldn't be pelted by ice.

I looked at my watch before I reached for the door handle. It was nine thirty. The event downstairs would be over. These post-work mixers never lasted long on weeknights.

"Aren't you leaving too?" I asked Daniel. Maybe I could explain myself as we shared an elevator down. Maybe he could explain it to her later.

"I am not," Daniel said pointedly.

Wasn't Bella worried about her safety? It was getting to be far too late for any unrelated man his age to be in her apartment, not without getting ideas on what he could do with her beyond networking.

"Who are you again?" I asked. Maybe he was an uncle or something, someone who'd keep her safe and not take advantage of her.

"Daniel Van Dijk," he said, as if his name was enough. For the first time I noticed his accent. Was he German or something else?

"Bella?" My "who is this and are you going to be okay" were wrapped up in that single-word question.

It was Isabella's turn to blush. "Daniel is...Daniel is..." she stuttered, then looked down, away. Her eyes refused to meet mine. "My sugar daddy."

"Bella!" Daniel yelled in reproof.

All that was jumbled in my mind sorted itself. Isabella was in a compensated dating relationship.

It wasn't the first one I'd heard of. My father's associates had mastered the art of that, with women in apartments scattered across the globe. Apartments like this one, only in Paris, London, Vancouver, Hong Kong.

But she'd gone to Owen. My dad had paid for it. So she didn't have debt like a ton of my classmates. Was she in this for a nice apartment and jewelry? She'd always been so self-contained.

"Why?"

"Because," she explained, like I was three fries short of a Happy Meal. "Your father refused to pay for Owen. He said he would, then cut me off when I wouldn't do exactly as he said."

"My dad isn't like that," I protested. He had always been an honorable, if ruthless, man in business dealings. Maybe not in his personal life. I was quickly trying to figure out if Bella slotted in the personal or professional when she spoke.

"Feng Wu is *exactly* like that. The car, the phone, the clothes. All of it was extortion. He paid. I kept silent about, well...you know what about. When he broke his promise to leave your mother for mine, I broke my silence. I was young and stupid, I'll admit. But he hit back, hard. Pulled the tuition blanket right out from under me. Just days past the financial aid deadline. I couldn't go home, so I did what I had to do."

What she had to do? No one had to sell themselves. That was the last act of a desperate person, not the first choice of a middle-class girl from New Jersey.

"Prostitution." I shook my head. Were there no women who did what they did for love? Was everyone working some kind of angle?

"Call it whatever you want, Jake. Your father made me the woman I am today."

"If you...I can't..." I didn't even know what I was trying to say. I'd lost the ability to articulate myself in English, something that hadn't happened in a long time. My head filled with Chinese. All that I wanted to say to express my outrage, my disgust at Isabella, at my father, at myself.

"Pick your jaw up off the floor and go home, Jake."

"What does your mother think?" I asked. Did Maria Aconi know? She couldn't. That woman would have dragged Isabella home to New Jersey by the hair if she found out.

"My very devout Catholic mother chose to stay with a man who's married. She chose a man who won't let me back on his property. She doesn't get a say anymore. Maria Sofia Aconi made her choice, and I made mine."

I looked between Daniel, whose face was now a mask of calm, and Isabella, whose face was a mask of indignant anger.

I shouldered my bag strap, pulled open the heavy door and walked out, making sure to slam it behind me for good measure. I needed to go home and figure out whether I could ever save Isabella from herself because if I dug down deep enough to places I didn't want to excavate, I knew this...all of this was my fault.

CHAPTER 19

FOUR YEARS EARLIER...

"AM I the only non-Chinese person here?" Abbott Gordon asked.

I shook my head. "My college roommate is here somewhere."

"I remember that guy. Cooper, right?"

"Cooper Warren. He's around somewhere. I think he said something about wanting to have a look at the view from the deck upstairs."

"I remember meeting him when you were a freshman. What happened to him? Did he graduate?"

I shook my head. "We weren't even in the Zuckerberg suite. We were downstairs, but he dropped out anyway."

"Dot com?"

I nodded. Bill Gates and Mark Zuckerberg had paved that alternate path from Cambridge.

"Which one?"

"Ones. He's gone through two IPOs."

"Wait. Let me guess." Abbott put his finger under his

chin and pretended to think deeply. "Ah, I know, now he's a venture capitalist."

"That's the flavor of it."

"My ears are burning. I know you're talking about me," Cooper Warren said as he strode into the hotel suite.

"Cooper, you remember Abbott. Abbott, Cooper."

The two guys shook hands. It only took two minutes before they started finding friends in common. I turned back to the mirror to adjust my tie. I'm not sure if it was my parents' or Liling's doing, but we were about to ascend to the sixtieth-story hotel dining room to an engagement party that would rival any wedding here or in the US.

Father hadn't understood why I'd needed anyone outside our families and their friends to come to this. I couldn't explain it to him. I just did.

Engagements in the east were nearly as big as weddings in the west. I didn't want to go it alone.

I very much needed Cooper and Abbott to give me some sense of normalcy like groomsmen did for a groom. They provided some sense that I wasn't going to disappear into the fabric of Nanjing or Shanghai, one in more than a billion, and never return to America, to the life I sometimes missed.

I'd been in China three long years. One working for Liling's father, seconded to Red Dragon. The other two learning the car business from the ground up. Design, assembly line, marketing, sales. I'd spent months in each department, immersed in all that was Woo DynoAutomotive.

"You're getting engaged in this big fancy party." Abbott patted me on the shoulder. "Honestly, I didn't think Lily would last."

"Last? She isn't an electronic part with a known useful life."

"She might as well have been. When did you fall in love with her?"

I punched Abbott in the arm lightly. "C'mon, man. You know how it is."

My boarding school roommate looked at me. Kind of tilted his head a little. Squinted. Abbott could do "bro" and "dude" as well as any guy. Underneath, he was sensitive, a thinker. He was more observant than he let on.

"Dude. I *don't* know how it is. You gotta tell me. When I was in Montenegro, I kind of fell hard for this girl."

"You did?"

"Yeah, I don't know. Didn't work out."

"Why?"

"Not sure. She was hot and cold. I sort of kept dating another girl in the program who I didn't like half as much. But that first girl...Milica was her name. Milica was like magic."

His tone was so sorrowful that I immediately thought of Bella. My heart stuttered for just a moment while the memory of her being that magic for me fogged my brain.

I shook it off. Thousands of miles, acres of regret, and what felt like a million years stretched between what had been and what was.

"So what are you doing very much single?" I turned the tables back to Abbott. He wouldn't let the focus stay on him, though.

"Man, I don't know. But does Lily...is she magic for you?"

"I'm going to pull the Chinese card here. That sounds

very Western. Voodoo magic and all that. Lily and I have a much more practical thing going on. Our families have always been close."

"Sounds like a merger."

"It kind of is. Marriage is about more than love. It's a financial institution. That's certainly been true in the east and the west," I started. "You studied Classics at Brown. I'm sure you could name dozens of families that were made this way."

His shrug was slow and deliberate.

"Man, if you're sure. I'm kind of holding out for the magic myself."

"Cooper! Get over here." He was at the window again, sizing up the view from our fiftieth-floor suite. "We have to get upstairs."

I bustled all of us out of the room and into the elevator farther down the corridor. Pushed the up button for the sixtieth floor.

I sucked in a breath before we stepped into the huge room. Panoramic windows revealed the growing skyscrapers that were dotting Nanjing's landscape, along with the tree-covered hills that made the city tolerable.

Red paper lanterns hung from the ceiling. Each table was covered in a gold tablecloth with red napkins on each plate. Western silver was side by side with chopsticks and a soup spoon. All the western trappings were becoming more and more popular with everyone I knew. As if using a fork and eating Italian or French food were the very height of sophistication. I'd played along to make Liling happy.

"Very red," Cooper observed. The front of the room had a

huge red velvet curtain adorned with the usual double happi-ness symbol that was at nearly every wedding.

"There you are," Min Li said as she rushed over to my little group.

"Mother, you remember Abbott and Cooper," I said.

"Yes, of course. You're good friends to come all this way," she said in her best English. "I'm glad that Jian...Jake knows such upstanding men." To me, she said, "Please come over here, so we can get ready." I followed her to a small room set aside for the families.

"Liling is nearly ready. She looks so very beautiful today. Be sure to tell her that."

"Of course."

"She's going to make a wonderful wife for you, you know."

"That's what everyone says."

"Love is one thing. It can grow over time. Loyalty...that's just as important, if not more. You need someone who will be with you even if there is misfortune. Do you understand?"

"Of course."

"There you two are. The guests are mostly here. It's time to start the ceremony," Father said. "This is such an auspi-cious day."

"I thought you didn't do fortune tellers and all that."

"I'm not sure I believe in any of it." Father's smile was surprisingly rueful. "We did consult with someone to make sure the engagement date wasn't *unlucky* at least. I'm glad this day worked out. Better to be on the safe side of the gods."

Min Li straightened my tie. It was the first time in years I remember her touching me or getting close. A feeling of something like contentment washed over me. It was the same feeling I often got when Liling made us dinner, or made sure my clothes were dry cleaned and arranged in my closet.

I lowered my head a moment. Americans would think I was praying. In a way, I was. I was wishing for, hoping for a sign that I was making the right decision. A head decision, not a heart decision.

Anytime I followed my heart, I'd gotten hurt. My father was a prime example of why that didn't work. Min Li, who clearly followed her head, seemed better off than the rest of us. I never saw her cry or wrestle with the decisions she made. She got up, smiled, kept each house in order. She was always impeccably dressed, surrounded by friends.

When the announcer called our names, I lifted my head. Min Li's smile. Father's smile...

My stomach knots untwisted. A feeling of utter calm came over me. That was the sign. This was the right thing to do.

I strode out with my parents, determined to make this the best engagement party our friends and family had ever attended.

CHAPTER 20

THREE YEARS EARLIER...

"YOU FOUND HER?" I'd only given the investigator the assignment a few days ago.

"It wasn't hard. It's not like she's a deadbeat dad hiding from the law," he said. I could hear his chair squeak over the phone, like he was leaning forward over a desk.

"And?" The anticipation was nearly killing me.

I'd tried. For one long year and a handful of days, I'd tried. I'd taken Liling to every party she wanted to go. I'd spent hours with Father's associates. I'd become an expert at both broadcasting and manufacturing.

It wasn't enough.

Abbott had planted a seed that day with his talk about the magical connection with that girl in Montenegro. It probably hadn't been his intention. But once the idea was in there, it was only a matter of time before it sprouted, before roots took hold.

I had to give it one more chance. I had to see if I could capture that magic...

With Bella—again.

"She's a director of Program Practices at CBT. She's in Los Angeles now. She left Philadelphia two years ago exactly."

"For the new job?"

"Not sure. Looks like an internal hire, though. The affiliate in Philly was an owned-and-operated. Which means the network owns the station. She probably applied and took the promotion out west."

"What does she do?" I couldn't tell from the job description he'd given.

"She's a network censor."

My steps faltered as I paced in the lobby of the hotel where I was having dinner. A censor was something I'd grown used to in China. All sorts of references were removed from broadcasts, mainly Tiananmen Square protests and references to the Free Tibet movement. It had been surprising to see those and other issues referred to when the Olympics had aired in America.

"The US has censors?" My teenage self had thought there weren't any censors at all.

"Not political, mostly sex and violence."

"Where is she living?"

"An apartment not too far away from her job. It's a high-density area with lots of single professionals."

"Is she...married?" It took a lot for me to ask that final question. I wouldn't have been surprised if she'd found someone else.

"Nothing in the public records. Do you want closer surveillance? These were database and records searches only.

Not the kind of thing to turn up a long-time live-in boyfriend."

"No. No. That won't be necessary." Liling was talking to the hostess. "I have to go. Please send the bill to me directly, not anyone at the company. Thanks for getting up early to talk."

"Let us know if you need anything further." The click of the phone from his end was a definitive close to our conversation.

I didn't need anything further. Not from the investigators. The rest was up to me.

"This is amazing," Liling said as she slipped on to the red velvet that covered the L-shaped booth in our private dining room. After we were seated, our host discreetly lit the candles at the table and handed us each heavy card stock, which listed the night's menu items.

The six-course menu featured duck, cod, and lobster. Handmade noodles and a rice-wine dessert rounded out the offerings. I'd picked this restaurant at the top of the Ritz Carlton with the hope that Liling knew how much I'd appreciated having her in my life.

"Come have a look," I said. I dropped my napkin to the antique wooden bench beside us, stood, and walked to the floor-to-ceiling windows. It was dark early, and the Bund was lit beautifully. Earlier rains had petered out, leaving a clear view of the old-style buildings from when European architects proliferated in the early twentieth century.

"Whenever I look at all these, I wish I'd studied up on architecture. They're more pretty than assertive. All the tall buildings in China are such a guy thing."

There did seem to be a race to have the tallest building. As soon as one was built, another would surpass it in Doha or Dubai, then another one would be built here.

We went back to the table when the waiter came and poured each of us tea and set the first course on the table.

I waited until Liling had selected pieces of duck skin and liver for herself before choosing one or two pieces for my own plate.

"Let me give you this before we start," I said. I placed my chopsticks down and lifted the small box from its matching glossy bag I'd brought with me from the corner of the couch.

"I didn't even see that red bag. Blended in so well with the cushions. Got me there." Liling smiled.

I pushed the package toward her. "Open it."

She extracted first the red leather box, then a softer velvet one inside. Finally, she slipped the gold bangle from the pouch.

Liling gasped. "It's the panther bracelet!"

"I saw you looking at it when we were in Cartier a few weeks ago."

I took the gold bangle from her and slipped it onto her wrist. The gold, garnets, and onyx gleamed in the soft light.

"I love it. Thank you."

"Happy birthday."

"I still miss you at work."

"It was only a secondment. It was good, though. I think it's given me a much broader sense of marketing now that I'm knee deep in cars."

"That's it? I think we were good working together. It was way better having you at Red Dragon. I keep hoping you'll change your mind and come back to entertainment. You have to admit its way more glamorous."

"Father's glad to have me back. We're looking at expansion and diversification in the US. It looks like I may go back and forth for a while."

"Mom's pressuring me for a wedding date. I was hoping we could pick one tonight." Liling snapped open her purse and pulled a folded sheet of white paper from it. "These are the unlucky dates," she said. She placed the stiff paper on the table so I could see it as well.

"Not you, too?"

"It makes the old people happy to know that we honored this tradition. My grandmother blistered my ear a few weeks back with all the stories of people who married on the wrong date. They lost businesses. Children died. Storms ate up their houses. You name it, it happened."

I kept up the small talk all through dinner. We talked about Liling's girlfriends. They were all, it seemed, buying up every luxury thing they could find in China, then traveling the world to find more. For Liling's sake, I was grateful she was nothing like her friends.

When I could finally calm my heart enough to speak honestly, I stood and went back to the window where I'd started the evening. Liling followed, and when she turned toward me, I took her hands in mine.

"There's something I want to talk about."

Immediately, she snatched her hands back. Her left arm was stiff in front of her while her right hand fingered her new bangle. "I don't like the sound of that."

"I think we should call off the engagement."

"Wait—*what?*"

"I'm not ready to get married," I said.

"You don't want to get married...or you don't want to get married to *me?*"

She'd hit the nail on the head with that one. I thought it was her, but there was no reason to share that. Nothing could be gained from hurting her like that.

"It's not the right time, Liling. Like I said, Father's ready to expand again. That's going to be me putting my head down. Taking lots of fifteen-hour flights. Not knowing where I'm going to be from one month to the next. That's not the foundation for a good marriage."

"Oh my God. Oh my God! I... Of all the things I thought you might say, I didn't see this coming."

She backed away and sat on the edge of the bench.

"I'm sorry," I said. "I didn't know a better way to tell you."

This had not been part of my plan when I was standing at the Cartier counter. It had not even been part of any plan when I'd made dinner reservations. But after that unexpectedly quick call from the investigator, my heart had turned on a dime. Following my head suddenly seemed like the stupidest thing I'd ever done. So I'd made a split-second decision. A heart-shaped decision that was starting to feel like the most ill-timed, ill-thought-out thing I'd ever done, even if it felt like the most right thing I'd ever done.

"Tell her what?"

I turned, startled at the sound of a third voice in the room. The host turned the lights up a bit. Enough for me to see that Liling's parents were coming into the room, followed by my own.

"Mr. Jiang. Mrs. Hsu..."

"Liling, are you crying? What's going on?" Mrs. Hsu and Mother rushed to her side.

"Liling and I are calling off our engagement," I said. "Work is very demanding right now. I was telling Liling that I think she needs to be with someone who can dedicate time to making a strong start to a marriage."

My father's eyes flashed, but he remained silent. When Min Li would have spoken, my father's hand on her arm kept her quiet. He wouldn't lie for me, repeat what he'd told me months ago, that he'd lighten my workload so I could establish a strong foundation with Liling, but he didn't want to ruin the relationship with Mr. Jiang, either.

"Are you seeing someone else? Is this about—"

"No. No, not at all," I said, cutting her off before should could invoke Isabella's name. After that night in my dorm at Harvard, Bella was an undercurrent in any relationship conversation or argument Liling and I had ever had.

Isabella had been a smoldering ember that had never been extinguished no matter how hard I'd tried.

"I think we're going to take Liling home," her father said. Looking toward my father, he said, "We will talk later."

They ushered my crying ex out of the private room. I was left alone with my parents. We were all silent for a long time. I didn't want to offer up a litany of excuses. They were all starting to sound lame even to my own ears.

"I have to go check on her," Min Li said. The sound of Liling's crying was like a faint melody in the room. They'd moved to another room or the hall, but hadn't left the hotel yet.

"What do you want, Wu Jian?" Father asked on a sigh.

"I think we need to diversify. Mr. Jiang is right about the media landscape. I don't think he's right about Red Dragon's future if he concentrates only on China. I learned a lot while I was there, though. We should consider purchasing something in America. Sony did it with movies and television. Bertelsmann did it with publishing. I think we can do it on the network level."

"Hmmm." I took heart that it wasn't an immediate "no."

"I want to go back to America to do it. I'll work with you at DynoAutomotive in New Jersey while keeping an eye on opportunities that come up. I'll be close enough to set up meetings in New York."

"Isn't this too different a business? Cars and appliances are not media."

"I've read up on GE's takeover of RCA. It successfully turned both NBC and Universal into global powerhouses. GE was known for light bulbs and washing machines before they bought one of the three major television networks."

"You have a point."

"I know this may have been easier with Red Dragon support. Maybe we can still do a joint venture with Liling's father…I don't know. But I do need to get back to America."

"Maybe it would be best for Liling and her family if you weren't here right now. The circle of our friends is small. She needs to be able to recover from her humiliation without seeing you at every party."

"Yes. Let me give her space."

"Isabella is not in New Jersey," he said. He'd turned away from me and spoken the last at the window.

I told my biggest lie yet. "What happened with Liling has nothing to do with Isabella, Father. One was a childhood crush. The other was some misguided sense of loyalty. We'd been together so long that it only seemed natural that we follow the next steps. That was wrong. She deserves someone who loves her. I'm not ready to be tied down. I want to have a hand in a possible new media venture."

"For once, Wu Jian, that makes sense."

"Do you want to go to Huaihai Middle Road?"

It had been years since I'd thought about that area of town. Years since I'd thought about the time my mother had been called a whore. A little solace of the female variety was starting to feel like it would be just the thing to block out the awful guilt of having done two women wrong.

"Why not?"

The hall was mercifully empty when we walked out. Wherever Liling and her entourage were, it wasn't here. The driver was at the front when we went down. Closed into the car, the noise of Shanghai disappeared. Quiet temperature-controlled air swirled around us. Father poured each of us two strong shots of baiju. I downed the first, then a second. I'd barely touched dinner, so the alcohol went straight to my head. That buzz did a lot to ease my conscience.

"How often do you go down there?" I asked as the car rolled through the thick traffic.

"Occasionally when I'm in town here. There's a woman who takes care of me. I'm sure there's someone for you as well."

My mind spun out as I started to wonder exactly what I'd see when I got to the end of the ride.

"Is it a house we're going to?"

"It's an apartment building. She has an entire floor. There are ten or twelve different women. There are even two who aren't Chinese."

Not Chinese. Like Maria Aconi. I usually shoved the fact of that relationship to the far recesses of my mind, to a place where I never visited. I wondered if his favorite was Chinese, like the wife he wasn't faithful to. Or Caucasian like the mistress he wasn't faithful to.

Neither one of them probably knew about this. They each thought the other was the problem. It was Father who was the problem, though.

I looked at his profile as he stared forward, probably thinking about the satisfaction that lay ahead for him. His face was one of a self-satisfied man who had the world in his hand. He could have everything that he wanted. There was little to stop me from being like him one day.

"How did you meet my mother?" I asked, loaded with the bravery of fermented grain courage.

"Why do you think about this?" He turned to me. With his glare, he said more than words. That I needed to let go of this once and for all because it made no difference, in his eyes, to my future, or what he was trying to achieve with his business.

"Because it's important to me. Because it's a part of my history that's missing." If he'd pressed, I couldn't have said why it was important. There was no logical reason to think that knowing some random facts about a woman who gave birth to me was somehow going to make any difference in my life.

Despite that, it mattered.

"There's nothing missing. Min Li raised you from birth. She's the one who took you from the hospital. Made sure you had the best food, the best clothes, the best schools. Those things are what made you who you are. Not the woman who incubated you for many moons."

"You were not adopted or raised by someone who wasn't your parent," I pointed out. "Why can't you just tell me this one thing? I'm not asking to meet her or for her address. I just need to know what happened."

"There are lots of kids who aren't raised by their parents. It's got to be a story as old as our great country."

"Are you going to answer? I'm so tired of dancing around this. Why can't you just tell me?"

"She was just a woman, Wu Jian. A woman who couldn't keep her baby."

The car slowed, then took a right as it slid into a space on a side street.

"Did you meet her here? What she really a prostitute?"

He'd slipped his cell up to his ear. I didn't know if he hadn't heard me or was ignoring me.

"They're ready for us. We can go up," he said.

I looked around. It wasn't quite Amsterdam's red light district, but there was nonetheless a combination of the usual businesses that catered to the drunk and horny. I may have been the former after those shots, but I wasn't the latter. Not with my father in the car and the mysterious facts surrounding my birth swirling in the air around us.

"I have no idea why I got into this car, but I'm getting out. Right here."

"Here?"

"I'll meet you at home," I said. Before he could protest, I opened my own door, slammed it, and stalked down the street and around the corner. I knew he wouldn't follow, either because he had his own agenda or because he wouldn't want to wade through the crowded street to find me.

It was surprisingly easy to disappear in Shanghai. I didn't know what I was looking for until I found it, neon sign pulsing against the night.

I walked into the tattoo parlor and talked to the first person I saw.

"I need a tattoo."

"To remind you of someone or to remind you not to make a mistake again?" the woman behind the counter asked.

"Are those the two kinds people get?"

"Sums it up. So which do you want?"

"A little bit of both, I think."

CHAPTER 21

NOW

STONE TEMPLE PILOTS. I was eighty-five percent sure that's what was blaring in Isabella's apartment. I had to marvel at her balls or chutzpah or whatever of paying off the rest of the people in the penthouses to give up their quiet enjoyment.

I'd wondered why she hadn't rented a house. Then I'd realized that Daniel probably used rent in this apartment as a means of control. Something that could be pulled out from under her at any second.

Every time I thought of Daniel, it sent me into a tailspin. Then I'd wanted to punch a wall.

For the last three weeks, I'd practically been cheek and jowl with Isabella. I'd taken a tiny office in her department. I saw her nearly daily. She treated me like any other coworker, with polite and cool distance.

Living and working in such close proximity was supposed to change her mind, convince her of my steadfastness. It wasn't working. My patience was worn out with waiting for something to change between us for her to bend the tiniest bit and acknowledge that there was something between us like there's always been.

I slipped into shoes, closed and locked my door and went to hers. If I wanted something to change, I needed to be the catalyst.

Knocking didn't work, so I banged until I got a response.

"Yeah, yeah," Isabella answered before she unlocked and opened her door. She did not look the least bit surprised to see me standing there. "I'll turn it down. Thinking about moving anyway. Don't think this place is my jam anymore."

Move? She was kidding, probably. Even in jest, the comment made my stomach twist and turn. I was glad I hadn't put any breakfast into it, otherwise I might have lost it all over her living room floor. My nerves nearly got the best of me, something that happened so rarely I needed to stop and figure out how to swallow the fear.

Twenty years, I'd known Bella. Twenty...and this feeling traveling through my body was worse than that day in the shed. Twenty years, and I was finally ready to make a go of it with the person I should have been with from the beginning.

"It's not the music," I said. I swallowed hard.

She looked everywhere but at me. Isabella looked...distracted.

"Your office not working out?" she asked when she finally focused on me again.

"The office is fine, Bella."

Her eyes cleared and she looked at me. She pulled her brows together. "Isabella," she corrected.

I took as deep a breath as I could take while not looking like I was terrified.

"You haven't said anything about us." I had to take in air, because I hadn't pulled in enough to not get light-headed. "Not since I—"

"There is no us." She looked away again. Down at her sneakers. Toward the inside of the apartment.

I took one cautious step inside. "There used to be."

"In two thousand one," she said. The gulf of nearly two decades yawned between us.

"So—"

"Jake. You have to...I don't know...go. Home. Across the hall or New Jersey or even China. China would be good."

As if six and a half thousand miles or ten thousand kilometers would make a difference to me. It had taken me two decades to realize that there was only one person for me.

"I'm not going back to China."

"Ever? Woo everything is there."

"I'm not going back today or tomorrow or until whatever this is between us is resolved."

Right then, a change came over her. It was something to see. Isabella's indifference vaporized like the morning clouds on a sunny Los Angeles day. She lifted her hand over my shoulder and pushed the door shut behind me. That same hand grazed my shoulder, my arm, then came down until our two hands were joined.

Her touch pulled me back in time to fourteen, fifteen, sixteen. The shed, the Led Zeppelin concert, the times we ran together to the woods just behind the house, the times we weren't afraid to touch because the family room's darkness shrouded us while blue TV light flickered.

She didn't have to pull hard. I would have followed her anywhere. Anywhere turned out to be up her short staircase to the loft bedroom where her unmade king-size bed stood like a beacon in the room, calling us to it.

I wanted her to be sure. I wanted this to be real.

"Bella?" I wanted her to acknowledge what was happening. For this not to be a fantasy I'd worked up in my head.

She didn't answer. Instead, her hand left mine and she fitted them against my shoulders. Her push was subtle, but I took the hint, letting myself sink onto the bed so I was sitting facing her. She didn't join me. Instead, she kicked off her tennis shoes.

Was she...? Were we...? Her pajama bottoms followed, and I think I got my answer.

I needed words. To be sure, I asked, "What are you doing?"

Her eyes went soft and shiny. I felt an answering tug in my own heart.

"I've missed you. For seventeen years, I've missed you. I'm done with that. Missing you, that is. You're here. I'm here. Let's be on the same page for once."

I had a complete answer in her next movement. Isabella folded her arms around herself like a hug and caught the hem of her tank. It came off next. I watched transfixed as her nipples got hard. I barely noticed as her underwear was freed. All her clothes tossed to a corner of the small room.

She wiggled her arms at her sides, then her gaze met mine.

"This is me," she said.

It was everything I'd always wanted and too much all at the same time.

"I thought we'd have lunch or something. I wasn't asking for this, Bella," I forced out.

"We've eaten a thousand meals together, Jake. Chinese. Italian. You taught me how to use chopsticks. I don't want all the pretense of forks, knives, and cloth napkins. I only want us."

Her argument was convincing. I'd never been so far from physical hunger for food in my entire life. My hunger for *her*, at that point, however, became ravenous.

I bent over, working to make myself as undressed, as vulnerable as she was. I'd only eased off my shoes and socks when I felt her feather-light touch on my shoulder.

"Let me," she offered.

In a near copy of one of the many fantasies where she's had a starring role, she knelt before me. Her fingers, as if they were acting of their own volition, lay against my hair, my eyebrows, against my closed eyelids. I tried to soak it up, live in this moment of the true connection I'd been seeking for so long.

I felt rather than saw the buttons of my shirt come apart, first one, then another, then the rest. Until this day, I probably wouldn't have been able to answer the question of how many buttons a man's shirt had or how many I closed on a nearly daily basis. Now I'd never forget. Never close a shirt again without thinking of Bella's fingers at my throat, on my chest, sweeping against my belly through my own tank.

I wanted to open my eyes and see. But more than that, I

wanted to feel. And feel I did. I was nearly light-headed when her hand hit my belt buckle. I could feel the heavy metal on my thigh. Then she unsnapped my jeans and eased the zipper down slowly, hindered by the bulge behind it.

"You're going to have to stand," she directed.

I opened my eyes to see her slowly rising in front of me like a mermaid resurfacing from the deep. She grasped my hand and I followed her lead and, in a moment, we were standing just apart. Impatient now, she shoved up my tank, and pushed down my pants, kicking all of it aside.

I was waiting for her to push down my briefs, make this all the more real. Instead she looped her arms around my neck. As if we'd done this a million times, my arms came around Isabella's waist and pulled her toward me. I hummed a piano concerto under my breath so softly, I didn't think she could hear, but she swayed to the tune anyway, laying her head against my shoulder.

We stayed like that a long time, until I couldn't. Until I was unable to stop myself from pushing my hips toward hers. In a moment, the air in the room took on a charged heat. Sweat prickled from my scalp. The hairs on my body seemed to rise, pull toward more of her instead of less.

I'd waited for so many years. I couldn't wait a moment longer. Neither could she. Her arms unwound and came to either side of my face. I lowered my head.

"Bella..." was the last thing from my lips before they met hers.

It was as if Chinese New Year and the American Fourth of July had come together in one big ball of celebratory fireworks.

It was better than I remembered. It was better than my fantasies. It was beyond my wildest dreams. Her lips were soft and yielding. Without hesitation, she opened for me.

She tasted like heaven. In seconds, I realized that I'd never get enough of her, not in this lifetime. Maybe not in the next. I wanted to believe in reincarnation, just so I knew we'd have a second chance do to this again, to be together.

When she pulled back, it wasn't because she was running away or I'd pushed her. I could tell that it was because she wanted to see me. I wanted the same, especially when her look was one of frank admiration and appreciation. I'd never felt more handsome or more appreciated than I did when her eyes feasted upon me.

It was only a matter of time before she noticed it, the one thing I'd hidden from everyone for years. She traced the tattoo on my arm. It was inked Chinese calligraphy style.

"Trust me, Father doesn't know."

"What is it?" Her finger on my arm was causing delicious shivers down my spine.

I didn't want to talk about the tattoo or what it meant. That was something for a more solemn occasion. Not today.

I moved my hand to the place I most wanted to touch. There was a freckle that I'd seen appear and disappear every summer, depending on what bathing suit or dress she was wearing. Now I could track a path from that tiny brown spot to the dusky nipple in the center of her swollen flesh. My mouth followed. I moved from one tip to the other, sucking and licking until she was squirming, her body craving satisfaction.

I slipped a hand between her legs, parting her flesh. We tumbled on the bed.

Mortification had haunted me more nights than I'd like to admit. My performance in my Woodward dorm room had been nothing to gloat about. I'd been selfish and plain unkind.

I rubbed her both fast and slow until her breath was coming in gasps. Until her moans filled the room. Until it was as it should have been that first time...our last time.

She gasped, moaned, then stilled. I removed my hand and stripped my briefs, tossing them to join the pile on the far side of the room. Isabella extracted a condom from a bedside drawer. I sheathed myself in on smooth motion, then moved so that I was over her.

I entered her before I'd thought to ask if she were ready. But she bit her lip as if it were the most delicious feeling, which it was. Better than I remembered. Better than I fantasized about.

Isabella was somewhere else. Her mind had gone to a place where I couldn't follow.

"Look at me, Bella."

She came back to me, to us. Her brown eyes met mine.

I let my weight settle on her, while I moved in and out, over and over again. "I never stopped loving you," I breathed into her ear.

Her eyes filled with unshed tears, and I wanted to make the pain of the past go away. I moved in her, willing us to make new memories to replace the old ones. I wanted to make it last. I didn't want it to end. But my body had other ideas. The pleasure became too much. I couldn't hold back.

In too short a time, I plunged into her one last time, grunting my release.

"That was...that was *everything*. I love you, Bella."

She turned her head—and I knew my honesty had been too much. But I'd been quiet too long, and at all the wrong times. I'd learned my lesson. She may not have been ready to hear what I said, but I had no regrets.

Before I fell asleep inside of her, I grasped the top of the condom and pulled out. The beauty of us having similar apartments was that it was easy to find her bathroom. I disposed of the condom, washed my hands, and came back ready for a long late-morning spoon. Maybe even a second time. I made myself comfortable against the padded headboard.

But Isabella had other ideas. She stood and wrapped herself in a waffle hotel bathrobe, which made me wonder what kind of resorts she'd visited, and who with. I shook my head, vowing not to go down that rabbit hole of jealousy, or regret at my decision to silently dump her all those years ago.

"I think you should go," she said.

My head was so tired, my eyes already drooping, so it took me a lot of seconds to figure out what she was asking—or maybe not asking, but insisting.

"Now?" Even more than I wanted sex again, I wanted to talk. Clear decades of air between us.

"Yeah, now. I need time..."

Time? As far as I was concerned, we'd had far too much time.

"To think about us?" I wanted to be together to talk about our future. I didn't understand her need to be alone.

"There is no 'us,' Jake." Her voice was so matter-of-fact that my post-orgasm high went away. Suddenly awake and alert, I turned to her.

"Are you saying there's no future for us?"

"I'm saying that I'm going to take a shower. Then do some laundry. Then I think I'm going to look at my calendar and put in for some vacation days. The controversy around Blue has died down a bit. The FCC will do whatever they do, but will take their time in doing it. Maybe I'll go to Paris. It's supposed to be beautiful in the spring. Or maybe Italy."

I was nowhere on that list. Not between laundry and vacation. Not between the FCC and Italy. This had gone off the rails fast, and I needed to set us back to rights. I could not let years of misunderstanding linger between us like it had in the past.

"Can we talk?" I moved at lightning speed, collecting and putting on my clothes. If we were going to have an adult conversation her way, I needed to be dressed for it. Armored up to combat her doubts. "Not here. Brunch. Where's good?"

"You know what? Brunch is a great idea. Meet me at the man door in thirty minutes."

I nearly crumpled in relief. I'd have time to have a real conversation in a place where she couldn't toss me out if she disagreed. Once I had my shoes on, I had a question.

"Man door?" Was there a woman door? It was moments like this that I questioned my fluency. There was always more English I didn't know.

"The gate. Thirty minutes," I heard rather than saw her say, because she was closing the door on me before she'd finished speaking those two words.

I went back to my apartment, sat on my couch, and counted to one thousand eight hundred. When it was time, I took the elevator downstairs to the apartment complex's Third Street exit.

She was there as promised, dressed like she was going to the gym. I think it was the most casual I'd ever seen her out of the house since she was fourteen and started making herself up like all the other girls. I'd never liked all the hairspray and eye makeup and tight clothes, but I'd loved *her*.

The man in a security uniform looked from me to Isabella and back, his demeanor that of a protective father figure. I wanted to tell him that Isabella was a woman who didn't need protecting.

"Ms. Aconi, you know Mr. Wu?" I tried not to show surprise that he knew my name. The good ones were like that, knew the residents. Kept a cautious eye on everyone else.

"We grew up together. Next-door neighbors. New Jersey."

"Imagine meeting up here! You're in the same building, right?"

"Neighbors. We're on the same floor."

"What a coincidence. That's fate." Suddenly, I liked this guy. If even *he* thought we belonged together, maybe I stood a chance.

"Right, Gerard. We're off to brunch to get reacquainted," Bella said.

He looked between us again, but this time his smile was different, wistful, hopeful. He pressed a hidden button, releasing the lock.

"Good eating," he said with a jaunty salute.

"Gerard? You know his name?" I wasn't so good with names.

"He's been here since the dawn of time." She frowned for a second, then whatever emotion she was feeling cleared from her face.

"The building is only fifteen years old or something like that," I said.

"There's an older complex in the back. Nearly everyone who's come to LA has lived there. It's called Park La Brea. I think he dates back to that era."

"I like that about you," I said. I wanted to grab her hand, hold it. Steer her around sidewalk panels broken by tree roots and teens wielding electric scooters, but it wasn't right yet. Not until we'd had "the talk" over brunch. Not until we were an established couple. But I was patient. I could wait. I'd waited all these years.

"Like what?"

"That you get to know stuff about people. You knew all this stuff about the Perez family. Remember them?"

"Are they still at Casa Wu?" she asked. That one took me back. It had been one of the names we'd used as a joke. Often when we'd come home from school, I'd say, "mi casa es su casa" as we split up between our houses.

"No, they retired a few years back. Moved back to some town close by."

"Brick." Once she said the name of their hometown, my memory was jogged.

"It's that kind of thing." I fiddled with the phone in my pocket, the walk-signal button. Anything to stop my hands from seeking out her touch. Patience, I told myself. There was still time. "Where are we going?"

"Farm to Table." Her pace was East Coast brisk. It was an effort to keep up. "They have a hangover special."

"You hung over?" Maybe that accounted for the casual way she was treating our morning, our oh-so-new couple status.

"Went to dinner last night in the Arts District. Probably had an entire bottle of white wine. Italian, so not too alcoholic, but still a whole bottle."

I tried not to be jealous. She had a life. She'd had a life without me for years. I wanted to be a part of it. I didn't want to go another day with her making plans I knew nothing about.

"Celebrating?"

"In a manner of speaking." Her turn toward a large glass door was abrupt. "This is the place."

I followed Isabella and the hostess, gratefully accepting the offer of the bottomless mimosa. She may not be drinking, but I could use all the courage I could get.

"Seltzer water for me, thanks," she said.

"So, how do you like the building? Good management?" I asked, trying to make small talk before the big one began. Trying to put her, but probably more myself, at ease. I couldn't remember the last time we'd had a normal conversation that wasn't laden with innuendo and shadows of our past.

"Are you asking about the apartment?"

"Sure. I've only been there a few weeks, maybe two months by now."

"Jake. This is a one-time-only thing, this meal we're having, so maybe you want to get to what you want to say. I'm happy to talk about Gerard and the nuances of the building complex, but it's probably not the best use of your time."

One time. I wasn't sure what she was talking about. Sex? Brunch? Both of those I wanted to repeat again and again.

I shifted my eyes toward the menu, hoping to make a choice and quickly dispense with the waiter. It wasn't to be. He went on and on about the chef's weekend masterpieces.

"Hangover special," Bella said. I think she hadn't been listening to anything the waiter said.

"Steak and eggs," I added. I knew the waiter was trying to do his job. Work for tips. I wanted to give him a hundred dollars to go away and never come back. I'd have done it, too, if I didn't think Isabella would be offended. But I suspected she would be offended, though. Growing up in that guest-house had made her hypersensitive about the differences between us.

"Didn't go bold," she said when I didn't elect for jalapeno foam or candied something or other.

"Never got used to sweet American breakfasts."

"You act like you haven't been here for the last twenty years." In her eyes, I was American. Had been since she'd defended me in middle school.

"I've been in Shanghai for the last six years," I said. In my mind, I would always straddle the line, not entirely comfortable in one place or the other. That discomfort had come, I thought, from not having Bella at my side. If I was here and she was with me, I think she'd turn Los Angeles or any place into home for me.

"Building cars?"

"Learning how to market cars, then working to start DynoMedia."

Isabella's "Mm" was neither conversation starter nor ender. I took a deep breath and got to it, the hard part.

"Have you thought about me? I thought about you all the time," I admitted. If there had been one constant thread in my life, it had been her.

"What did you think...about me?" she asked. I could see the gears turning in her mind. her wondering what judgments I'd made. Truthfully, there were many. But those had come from an immature mind. I knew better now. I could see how our lives were more different than the same I'd thought they were those years past.

"I wondered how you were."

"How...I...was..." She hesitated a long moment, as if wondering how to spoon-feed it to me. I deserved every moment of that hesitation. "I graduated from school, had a series of jobs, ended up at CBT." When I didn't say anything, she ended with, "I was fine."

"Are you dating someone?" I asked. Even if she was, I was ready to ask her to choose.

To choose me.

"Now, you ask. Not before your big declaration of intention, but now?"

My timing hadn't been the best. Ours never had, but none of that mattered. *We* could overcome anything. We could move past her Dutch billionaire. Because of course I knew who Daniel was. Had tracked his every corporate move since that night in Philadelphia. I wasn't competing with thirty-year-olds with middle-management jobs and entry-level luxury cars. I was competing with a man who'd had a fifteen-year hold.

"*Are* you free?"

"You're asking about Daniel. About whether I'm still sleeping with men for money?"

"I wasn't going to put it exactly like that," I said plainly. I didn't have the ability to sugarcoat it anymore. I was going for broke.

"Why skirt it? No, Daniel and I broke up once and for all."

"When?" I tried not to sigh and collapse on the table with relief. Jump for joy.

"Last night."

"Oh. So there's hope for us. I was thinking it was going to be so much harder than this."

Isabella hadn't cleared much of her special when she leaned down to get her purse. I nearly panicked when I thought she was going to leave. Instead, though, she extracted a long cream-colored envelope. I couldn't imagine what a CBT envelope had to do with hangovers, or brunch, or...us.

"What's this?" I took what she offered and flipped it back and forth. It was thin, like it only held one piece of paper.

"Maybe you should open it." Her tone made me stop fidgeting with the thick paper.

"Why do I feel like I shouldn't?"

"I'm handing this to you as Vice President of Program Practices at CBT," she said, her tone formal. "I've already sent this same letter to HR and my direct boss via e-mail."

Curiosity got the best of worry. I slipped in my finger, careful not to get a paper cut, and lifted the flap.

"I hereby tender my resignation from my position as Vice President of Program Practices for CBT, effective immediately..." I read out loud, then dropped the letter on the table once my brain caught up with what I was seeing. "Not even two weeks?"

I felt like Kiefer Sutherland in an episode of that terrorist show where every decision had to be instantaneous. Real life didn't work that way, except now when it did.

"When I started here, I jumped the line," she said plainly. "Connor Quinlan can step into this job tomorrow and probably be much better at it than I."

"So this is it?" I was disappointed, sure. But if I'd learned anything in life, it was that organizations can go on without one employee, one department, even one CEO. They had a life of their own.

"I'm sure CBT will be fine without me."

"And us?" I asked, though I was starting to think I could guess the answer. My hunger again vanished and I pushed aside my steak and eggs.

"This isn't our time."

"Are you serious?" My question was a definite push back.

"Deadly. It's not that your offer isn't appealing. But I can't be bought."

"I'm not trying—"

"CBT. FCC fines. You're probably a billion-plus into the hole on this one."

"Good investment strategy—"

"Dictates that you want a return. I hope you get one.

Keep CBT pushing the envelope and you'll be golden. As for me...I think I need closure, and I can't get it here."

"Is there hope for us?" I know the question wasn't manly or strong, but I needed to know the answer more than I needed to protect my ego.

It was so obvious now that what had happened those hours before had been a pity fuck. Or a nostalgia fuck. It had not been what I'd wanted it to be...making love. A new start.

Isabella's shrug was an answer. Her gathering her gray Burberry trench around her like a hug was an answer. Her pitying smile before she stood and left the restaurant was an answer.

Her answer was no.

I had no idea where I'd go from here.

❦

Thank you for reading **WHAT WAS LOST.**

I loved this book so much. Isabella is my heart. **WHAT WAS TRUE** the last of the trilogy is out now.

If you love crazy, beautiful, love stories, then you'll want one-click TAMING THE BAD BOY now!

Sometimes good girls do bad things... Can Ivy League Daisy tame bad boy comedian Raphael? Or is Ivy League out of his league?

"Read it. Loved it. The depth of characterization is beautiful. The story feels rich and real. Two flawed individuals that fall in love and must overcome their own personal challenges and resistance to love."

—*USA TODAY* BESTSELLING AUTHOR
MAGGIE MARR

ABOUT THE AUTHOR

I write crazy, beautiful love stories because I believe story-telling is magic. I love complicated heroines with secrets, strong heroes who fall hard, and a long winding road to happily ever after. When I'm not writing, I love to travel to witness the diverse tapestry of humanity, photograph the beauty of the world, visit museums, and watch live theater. I live in West Hollywood, California.

xo Jolie Moore

♥

I haven't found my own happily ever after, but I'm not done trying. This year I'm going to go on fifty first dates. Join me as I try to find my Mr. Right or maybe Mr. Right Now. #50first-dates #joliemoore #crazybeautifullove

Sign up here to get weekly date updates as well as new release notifications.

joliemoore.com/50firstdates